THE PERFECT SACRIFICE

THE
PERFECT SACRIFICE

ABBI GORE SPIVEY

PALMETTO
PUBLISHING
Charleston, SC
www.PalmettoPublishing.com

Copyright © 2024 by Abbi Gore Spivey

All rights reserved

No portion of this book may be reproduced, stored in a retrieval system, or transmitted in any form by any means–electronic, mechanical, photocopy, recording, or other–except for brief quotations in printed reviews, without prior permission of the author.

Hardcover: 9798822973602
Paperback: 9798822973619
eBook: 9798822973626

To Myself,
Who went through too much, too soon.
Thank you.

Trigger Warning:
This book contains the following: violence, death, drug use, alcohol use, abuse, homophobia, adult language, and adult themes.

PROLOGUE

Hurting people was a good pastime for me. I enjoyed the chaos and the haywire emotions that I caused. My life was as smooth as could be, and everything worked out the way it had to. A balancing act between me, evil, and everything else good; or somewhat.

Everyone has a darkness in them, something that breaks through the skin and shows their true colors. I was always selfish. If something didn't benefit me, or even if I just didn't feel like dealing with it, I simply wouldn't participate. I never cared about how I was viewed, or even tried to be welcoming, until I met her.

My dark haired beauty who tested the grip on my patience and who made me stumble for words. She was good. She cared about people; the world seen through her eyes truly showed the epitome of naivety in this world.

I like to think she looked at me with softer, more delicate eyes when she saw a smidge of good in me.

But she believed everyone could be good, and she learned—the hard way—that isn't always the case.

It was hard being the villain and being in love. Especially when someone like *me* is in love with someone like *her*. I'm the bad guy, and unlike the good ones, I would've burned down the world for that goodbye kiss.

ONE

Samara

The vibrations from my phone on the nightstand snap my eyes open, the nearby lights flood my vision. "Hello?" I answer my phone with a raspy voice.

Francis' peppy voice comes over the speaker. "Sam! Get down to Subway Station Twenty-Three! There's been a murder!" As gruesome as murders can get, Francis is as peppy as ever. Reporters in this city are like starving dogs and whenever something big happens, it's like waving a steak in their face.

"On my way." After hanging up, I catch a glimpse at the clock. 2:43 a.m. I would've had to get up for work in two hours anyways.

I throw the covers off and walk right into the bathroom while checking the weather to see what I should wear. Glancing back through my room and out the glass that lines my far wall, I see it's not raining. I put my voluminous raven hair into my signature low bun and head out towards the den. Leaning down by the door for my boots, I begin to slip them on as Camille sits up from the couch.

"Where are you going?"

"Got a call from Francis about a murder at a subway station."

She stands up and walks over to the fridge, "Sounds juicy."

Her small afro bounces as she walks, and even though she just woke up, she's still such a beautiful kid. Camille is sixteen, and I take her in every now and then, depending on her situation at home. I could say something about being her savior, but she actually saved me.

Over three years ago, I was a fresh twenty-two year old who just graduated from college and moved to a new city to start my job. I definitely didn't know my way around then, and there's still a lot about this city that I don't know. Camille, however, knows this place like the back of her hand; even though she's almost ten years younger than me. I had taken a few wrong turns and found a couple drunk guys in an alley. Camille grabbed my hand and got me out of there before they could lay a hand on me.

Ever since then, we've gotten closer, and at times, she's lived here for months before she heads back home. Her dad, Bradley, is a drunk and her Mother passed away when she was just a kid. I always ask if he's ever hurt her and she always says no. But, just because he's never harmed her, doesn't mean she has no reason to be scared of him.

"He called again." She hops on the counter as she opens her water and stares at me. "Dad called again." I sigh as I zip up my boot. I know she doesn't want to, and frankly I don't want her to, but she should go home and check in.

"You should just drop by and see him." She shakes her head and begins to speak but I hold up a finger, "I know you don't want to. Just go home and check in to get him off your back. Then, come back here. He's only allowing you to stay here because he knows I feed you and keep you safe."

She lets out a breath and nods. "If he knows you take care of me then why do I have to go back?"

"Because I'm not legally your guardian, and he can take you and make sure we never see each other again." She slumps against the counter in defeat. "I don't think either one of us wants that."

She shakes her head and replies, "Okay, I'll go sometime today."

I nod and smile softly, "Good. I'm headed out. Go back to sleep, it's early." I wave her off as I grab my purse and head out the door. Before the door shuts I hear her say, "Good luck!" I'll definitely need it.

Getting to the train station took no time considering it was close to my apartment building. As I get to the stairs that lead underground, I see Francis being escorted out by police.

"Okay, okay! I'm leaving, get your hands off of me." The two officers let her go and she brushes off her coat. She looks up to see me and runs over to me. "Sam!"

"Francis, I'm sorry I didn't make it in time."

She shakes her head. "Forget it." At first, I think she's mad at me, I would be too. Now that the police are here, we can't go in or we risk getting arrested. "Look." I blink. She's holding her phone in front of my face with pictures of the crime scene. My mouth falls agape as I grab the phone from her. She comes to stand beside me so we can look at them together. I glance around first, making sure no police officers or bystanders are lingering.

I start swiping through her phone and my intake of breath doesn't go unnoticed. "It was gruesome, I had to hold my breath while I was down there." The pictures show a female, probably early to mid twenties. She's got platinum blond hair and her clothes are ripped to shreds.

"That looks like,"

"Claw marks." Francis finishes my sentence as my mind swirls. The victim is lying on her stomach, and large claw marks have ripped through her back. I continue to swipe through to a picture of her face. I gasp as Francis has to look away. "It was so bad, Sam. Who could've done something like this?" The picture shows her structured face. High cheekbones, a sharp jawline, and I'm sure what were beautiful eyes. Except, I won't ever know, because they aren't there anymore. All that's left is a blank, black cavity of emptiness. Blood streams stain her face.

"It looks like she was crying," I say to Francis without even looking away from the photos. I continue to swipe, my empty stomach begins to turn.

"All right," Francis' voice drags me out of my observation, "let's get to reporting." The van for the company, Shapiro Informatics, pulls up and the news crew gets out. I nod, and let Francis position me the way she wants before she starts doing what little bit of makeup I need.

The rest of the early morning was a blur. I don't even bother heading home. Instead, I just make my way to work. The streets are busy by the time we are done filming. The clouds begin to hang over the top of the building, and the sun doesn't shine through. With events like last night, I wouldn't expect it to.

TWO

Rowan

As I stand on top of one of the many buildings in New York City, the breeze from the harbor blows my hair around and wafts the salty smell towards me. The wind makes me feel like I'm flying, I wish I could right now. "Rowan!" I turn and see Mekaia. "What are you doing here?" Mekaia looks similar to me; black hair, tall, and sturdy build, except his eyes. My eyes are blue, while his are green. Although, lately he's been having trouble seeing, and sometimes I see one of his eyes as a red color. Everytime I bring it up, he just changes the subject. "I need you to monitor lower Manhattan tonight. It's your turn."

"Well, what about you?" He chuckles at my question as he comes to stand beside me. We overlook the buildings and lights together in silence for what seems like a long time.

"I need a night off."

That's unusual. Mekaia is always working, always leading us. "What's wrong?" He shakes his head and looks back at me.

"No, I'm fine. I just thought tonight would be a good time to take a break. It's been awhile since I've relaxed." I chuckle and nod my head.

"Alright, I'll go ahead and take off." I've never had to be formal with him, but he grabs my arm as I turn to leave, and I look at the connection. When our eyes meet, it's like he's letting off a dark glow. I lower my gaze, it's not a challenge. "Sorry, I didn't realize you were so stressed."

He slowly lets go and runs his hands through his hair. "Rowan," As he trails off, I return my gaze to him and see his eyes are glassy, and the red color has returned.

"Mekaia," He looks down over the side of the building. "Go rob a store or mug a grandma. Be selfish, be chaotic. After that, go home. Take a break." I pat his back, feeling the ridges that let his body change.

"Maybe you're right." I nod as his head rises and his body relaxes. I can tell his eyes have returned to normal.

"I'll be going now." I wait for his approval, trying not to worry about another episode surfacing.

He slightly nods his head and says, "See you at home." After that, I take a step off the building, and let my wings be free. Flying feels so great, feeling the wind between my wings and the chills gliding through my body never get old.

We usually divide up the boroughs and patrol on night shifts. There's usually anywhere between five to ten of us monitoring each borough. I don't usually do it, but since Mekaia asked me, I guess I should suck it up. During the day we have less people patrolling, but it's always happening.

Our largest population is in New York, problems are a possibility, and sometimes they arise. Our large population can attract other supernatural beings and the order has to be maintained. This is our city, and every other supernatural being that passes through, or stays, is required to report to us. If they don't, then they can wreak havoc on our territory and cause imbalance. It's like the saying, too much of something is a bad thing.

My black wings stretch out and feel the wind catch under them, lifting me higher into the air. I make sure to stay clear of the extremely tall buildings and continue watching from above the smaller ones. I see a dark figure leap across the buildings and I squint to try to get a better view. It leaps again and I continue to try to figure out what it is. With no luck, I lower myself closer to the buildings.

Once I get closer, it disappears, so I land on top of one of the buildings. Walking around the roof to find any clues, I see that there's a clump of black hair resting near the edge of the roof. As I pick it up and rub my fingers over it, it feels more coarse than regular hair. Fur?

A distant smell of blood begins to hit my nose and my head whips in the direction of it. Right below the building is an entrance to the subway. I jump off the edge and let my wings gently guide me down. Once my feet touch the ground, my wings retract and make rips in my shirt, to my dismay. I walk towards the subway entrance, and the smell of blood grows.

It's still dark outside, I'm not sure what time it is; but it's the sweet spot when no one is out. Walking down the stairs to the subway, I see drops of blood leading deeper into the station. I follow the blood and realize the farther that I get into the station, the bigger the puddles get. All of a sudden, they stop. I look around and the station is completely empty. Eerily empty.

I continue to walk through the station until a scream rips through the emptiness and down my spine. It quickly stops, like it was cut off during the middle. I hurry towards the source of the scream and see a black figure rush out from around the corner. I chase it without hesitation and we head down the empty train tracks. Whatever it is, it's fast, so fast that I can't even make out what it is. It's just a big blur that I'm losing my momentum on. A train light begins to head my way, and whatever it was, it must have found its way to the abandoned tunnels that run under the city. It leaps to the side and disappears. I grunt in frustration and then turn around as my wings spread out quickly to get me out of the way of the train.

When I return to the station, I go back to the corner where the object ran out from. A woman, probably in her mid-twenties, is lying dead on the cold tile floor. I know whatever did this wasn't human, just by looking at the claw marks on her back. Her shirt is ripped and it looked like claws went right down to the bone. I change positions to get a better look and see that her eyes are gone and blood streams down her cheeks. She was crying. Blood surrounds the nearby floor and I begin to hear shuffling coming from the same entrance I came in.

I hide behind a nearby pillar, my slender but sturdy frame fitting perfectly behind it. A small woman with a blonde bob and thick glasses comes around the corner carrying pepper spray. Someone probably called it into the police when they heard the scream.

She's probably a reporter, I'm not sure what pepper spray would do against a murderer, but whatever floats her boat. I can tell that she can't stand the smell and that she's holding whatever's in her stomach down. She pulls out her phone and starts to take pictures of the body. Greedy. Always trying to get the first scoop on a kill. My kind may be evil, but we don't kill humans. They're greedy enough to do that themselves.

Soon enough, the cops show up after she gets a few more pictures. "Ma'am, you're not supposed to be here." Before she can resist, the officers take her by the arms and begin to lead her out. While the subway is still empty before they get everything blocked off, I walk out the other side of the station. I turn to see the woman meeting with someone.

"Sam!" She yells at the woman walking up.

"Francis, I'm sorry I didn't make it in time." Francis shakes her head and holds up her phone to Sam.

"Forget it. Look." No doubt showing her the pictures. I see Sam take a breath in and I know the images are disturbing to her.

I walk over to the edge where a building meets with the sidewalk to hide behind, keeping an eye on the two women as a van pulls up and Francis starts putting makeup on Sam as she begins to record a report.

"The police received a call from a bystander at 2:38 a.m. reporting a strange scream that started and quickly stopped in the subway station. When the police got here, they discovered a Jane Doe, with what appear to be claw marks stretching from her neck to her lower back."

She continues to report whatever she knows to, understanding that they'll probably use this for notes or until the police start conducting an investigation. I turn the corner and spread my wings, flying up all the way through the alleyway. I have to head home and tell Mekaia.

THREE

Samara

"Sam," I look away from my computer and turn to the side of my cubicle, "I heard you got details on that Jane Doe murder?" Joshua Mintz has always been a thorn in my side. We were hired about the same time and are in a serious competition for approval. He's definitely got some superiority/inferiority issues. His brown eyes are always dull, except when he's reporting or getting the scoop. Dark brown hair lies against his tan skin and his teeth are so straight you can tell he had braces when he was younger. He'd be handsome if he wasn't such a prick.

"See anything good?" His question makes me sigh and shake my head.

"I didn't get there in time. Francis was being dragged out by the cops whenever I got there."

He laughs but I can tell it's not a hearty one. "Tell Francis if she wants a reporter who actually helps, to come to me." I give him a glare as he walks back to his cubicle. As I roll my eyes, the phone begins to ring. As I answer, I can already hear Francis talking to someone near her. "Samara Allen speak-"

"Sam!" Yanking the phone away from my ear, I can still hear her perfectly. She's not really one for whispering. "I have bad news, we need to meet and talk. Have you had lunch yet?"

After agreeing to go to lunch with Francis, we met in the lobby and headed to a nearby cafe. "What news is so important that you have to tell me in person?" We move up a space in the line as she shakes her head.

"You need to be sitting down for this."

"Unfair. You know I get anxious." She nods and looks at me through her thick glasses.

"This is something everyone should be anxious about." A lump forms in my throat by the time we get to the counter. Francis ends up ordering something with lots of details, and I just get a black hot coffee and a bagel.

After sitting down at a table by the windows, Francis lets out a breath and starts talking. "I overheard Mrs. Shapiro on the phone when I went by her office." Catalina Shapiro, owner of Shapiro Informatics, is a very strong and frightening woman. "She was talking about how she was going to start making cuts." My heart sinks to my stomach. "Apparently, the deadline is almost up, and she's decided to go ahead and start crossing out people." I knew when I accepted the job that it was a high risk for termination. The reporting world changes daily and a company can only have so many employees. There are fifty people in my specific department on the same level as me. Unfortunately, there will only be twenty after Ms. Shapiro makes her cuts.

"What will I have to do to stay?" The only thing left for me in the small hometown I come from is my Mother. No job, no prospects, no future.

"You need to get a story, and a big one at that."

"What about Jane Doe?"

Francis shakes her head. "I haven't heard anything else about it. I don't think the police are trying to go too public with it right now. Probably don't want to cause panic." With Francis' pictures and what the police do release, I could eventually start my own investigation into this.

"Will you text me those pictures that you took?" She nods and sends them to my phone as she takes a sip of her coffee.

"For the record, I hope you make it through. You're a joy to work with." Francis has always been nice, and it's no doubt that she takes her work very seriously.

"Thanks, Francis." She doesn't bother nodding, and begins to lean closer to the window, looking out to the crowd of people who are forming in front of the building across from the cafe. I follow her gaze and see everyone looking up towards the top of the building.

I rise from my seat and run outside. "Francis, video!" I tell her and she grabs out her phone, ready to get whatever she can. Once we are outside and making our way through the crowd, I get a better view of a man on top of the roof. His back is to the edge and someone is holding him by his shirt. Their face is covered so you can't see who it is, but he raises his hand like he's about to hit the person. "Francis, up there!" Her phone raises with her gaze and she zooms in as far as she can go.

The man on the edge of the building is hit across the face and then he stops moving, the wind blows gently but sounds like a train over the sound of screams throughout the crowd. A knot forms in my gut as the person lets go of the shirt, causing the man to fall from the building.

I turn away and cover my ears. The only thing I can hear is the screaming from those surrounding us and then a quiet car alarm. After a couple seconds, I remove my hands from my ears and the car alarm becomes louder. Francis is the first to rush forward, her need to capture a story burning through her skin. I follow behind her slowly as I hear people behind us calling the police. "Sam," Francis' voice cracks as I reach her side. She backs up to let me see. The person wasn't hit across the face, they were scratched, deeply. The skin that encloses the side of his mouth is ripped open, and one of his eyes is gone. However, that's not the thing that draws me in. There's a hole in his chest, and it looks to just be an empty cavity. Looking back up to the building, I no longer see the man.

"Sam, where are you going?" Francis yells at me but I'm moving before her words register in my head. He has to be coming down in the elevator or the stairs. Running through the lobby, the elevator closes to go up before I get there. I don't have time to wait. I run to the stairs entrance and begin my ascent to the top. The building is smaller, so there aren't as many stairs. Halfway up I decide to take off my heels so I can make better time. I burst through the door to the roof, my breathing is fast and the phone in my hand feels heavy; I'm ready to get any evidence I can.

Except there's nothing, no one is up here. I slowly walk further onto the roof, to where the man was standing. A pool of blood sits in his absence, and droplets of blood go to the opposite side of the roof. I follow them, trying to trace where the unknown man could have gone. Except, the droplets lead off the side of the roof, and there is no sign of anything else. The wind blows my hair back as I try to get a hold of my breathing "What the hell is going on?" The wind carries my unanswered question to no one in particular.

FOUR

Rowan

"Where's Mekaia?" After returning early this morning, I couldn't find him anywhere. I specifically told him to get some rest and he just goes off on his own.

"I saw him head out not too long ago. Why? Lovers quarrel?" Rose walks up behind me and slaps my shoulder. Her pale skin and green eyes always intimidate me a little bit, just because I know how badass she can be. Not to mention she's drop dead gorgeous.

"Something's happened and I need to report it directly to him."

She sighs and runs her hands through her red hair. "You know how incident reports work. Give them to Uriah and he will give them to me. I'll be sure to get it to Mekaia."

I shake my head and step up closer to her, "Rose, I don't have time for this. It's urgent."

She pokes out her lip and says, "It's definitely a lovers quarrel." She turns on her heels and begins to walk away. I turn the opposite way until I hear her say, "He said he had some business to take care of. I'm not sure where he went. Sorry, Rowan."

Her saying my name sends chills up my body and I look over my shoulder back at her, "It's fine, I'll find him on my own. Thanks." I walk out of the abandoned subway station deep underground. This is just one of the places that we have to stay.

As I reach the exit, Mekaia walks in, looking refreshed. "Where have you been?" I ask him with a tone of authority in my voice.

He looks at me and smirks, "Come on. I went and got some rest and now I'm feeling better."

I turn to head back down with him. Changing the tone in my voice, "We need to talk," I make it known that this is a serious matter. He follows me and we return to where I started. Passing Rose, she lowers her head when Mekaia passes. Just because I don't have to be so formal with him, doesn't mean everyone else can. I open the door to his office for him and wait for him to enter first. Once we are in his office, which is really just the front cab of an abandoned subway train with a desk in it, he sits while I close the doors.

"What is so urgent?" To any other person, it would've sounded like he didn't care, but I knew better. He was a strong leader and he cared about every single one of us.

"Are you aware of any werewolves passing through the area?" The look on his face tells me that this was the last thing he was expecting.

"Werewolves? What happened?" I pull out one of the chairs and sit, letting out a deep breath.

"A girl was murdered early this morning in a subway station. Claw marks all the way down her back and black fur at the scene," I run my hands through my hair and look down, "I was on patrol and I saw something. I just couldn't catch it fast enough, it got away underground."

Mekaia shakes his head and stands up, turning to face the open glass of the cab. "It's not your fault. I know you, and I know you tried your hardest." After a moment of silence, both of us thinking of what new steps to take, Mekaia turns around and faces me. "I will alert the normal patrollers to establish a perimeter. The ground patrollers will get whatever information they can in regards to recent supernatural passings," pulling files out of his desks, he continues to speak, "We, the fallen angels, are the biggest cluster of supernatural beings in New York City. This is our territory. Make sure any supernatural creature knows they need permission before passing through." His breathing increases as he continues to talk and I try to avoid eye contact as much as possible. Catching a glimpse at him, I see that one of his eyes has returned to the red color I fear so much. "When we catch this trespasser, everyone will know that."

I nod, "As you say."

Keeping my head low to the ground and listening to his breathing slow down, he plops down in his chair once again, and runs his hands over his face. "Rowan, I need you to go see what you can find out." His voice has returned to normal, and his eyes have turned back by the time our gazes meet. I nod and excuse myself.

Before closing the doors, I turn back and say, "Don't worry, Mekaia. I'll take care of it." He smiles and motions for me to close the door with his hand. As I walk back out and pass Rose, she looks at me with a questioning glare. "Get him the records of the supernatural beings that pass through our territory. Let the patrollers know to look for any supernatural being that doesn't have clearance, and bring them directly to him." She nods and gets to work as I walk out and up to the surface. The entrance to Mekaia's hideout is through an abandoned building. No one ever comes here, besides the usual troublemakers. It's still pretty early in the morning, but the streets are flooded with people as everyone's day begins. I decide that it's probably best to walk, since the skies aren't cloudy enough for me to fly.

I walk down the street, trying my best not to run into anyone. Thoughts fill my head about what's happening and what it means.

Fallen angels, it sounds so hardcore. We're really just a bunch of outcasts, shunned by the Heavenly angels for wanting more out of life. Who really knows though, once you're cast out, all of your memories are wiped. Not Mekaia, though. He's the only one who can remember what it was like up there. The reason Mekaia is our leader is because he's strong and knows how to lead well. However, he's also the oldest fallen angel ever known. I think that's why he can remember his life from before, because he was the first one.

I'm over five hundred years old, but there's no telling how old he is. We look the same as we did in Heaven, and we don't age, plus our senses are heightened. Pretty much a prehistoric vampire with wings.

When you're cast out, it feels like a void in your chest that you can't replace. We were ripped from our home, just because we wanted more. Since Mekaia is the oldest and retained his memory after banishment, he's all knowing, and can answer any questions we have about what happened. When he found me, I was afraid and I felt no warmth, until his understanding flooded into me and I felt at home again. After being on Earth for a couple decades, I finally got the courage to ask him why I was cast out.

"You were in love. You put her first."

His words struck a chord in me and I refused to believe it. Knowing that something as simple as love could have been the reason for my banishment made me resent the feeling of it all together. After knowing, I locked the part of me that could care for anyone in any other way than loyalty. I have friends that I would protect, like Mekaia and Rose. But, the feeling of love,

I've never known it in this life. I once asked Mekaia about his reason, but he shut me down and got the same look in his eye when he was talking about the trespasser. It's better to leave him when he looks like that.

A continuous string of walking and thinking lead me to a local supermarket. I snag an apple from one of the stands where the vendor isn't looking, and continue on my way through. Coming out at the other end, I see a group of people gathering in front of a building. I look up with them and all I can make out is what looks to be someone who is going to jump. Looking back down to the crowd, I see two people pushing through, one with their eyes on the roof and one with their phone out. Probably reporters.

"Francis!" I hear one of them yell and remember the name of the person who first got to the crime scene last night. I see the blonde woman, Francis, and she is the one holding the phone, and the one who called out her name, what's her name again? I look up to the top of the building and see that the jumper is being held by someone. I can't make out who it is because their face is covered. The building isn't that tall, but a fall from that height is fatal. In an instant, the person holding onto the jumper slaps him across the face and then grabs him again. Except, the smell of blood begins to leak into my nostrils as his hand lets go of the jumper, and he falls backwards off the building.

Looking back to where those two reports are, I see Francis still videoing as he's falling, while the other turns around and covers her ears: innocent, afraid of death. A car alarm sounds as the jumper's lifeless body slams on top of a nearby vehicle. The two reporters lurch forward to investigate, and I take the opportunity to run across the street and to the side of the building. Luckily, the building and the one next to it meet at a small alleyway, so there's no foot traffic through it. I spread my wings and begin to ascend to the top of the building, it's the fastest way to get there. I reach the top of the building quickly, and find no one else on top of the roof. The smell of blood comes from a puddle where the jumper was standing. The man with the mask wasn't holding onto him, he had his hand inside him.

I look down over the top of the building and see the two reporters near the jumper. I focus on his face and see that he's been scratched, just like the girl from last night. This was another attack by the trespasser, except this time, the only trail he left are blood droplets off the side of the roof. Where could he have gone?

I hear Francis yell, "Sam, where are you going?" Sam must be the name of the other reporter with her. Knowing that she's probably coming up here to see if the perpetrator is still here, I hide behind the door from the staircase that enters onto the roof. A minute or two goes by and the door bursts open, revealing a heavy breathing reporter. Her hands clasping her phone tightly, she walks out onto the roof. I observe her quietly. She follows the same trail I made, walking towards the pool of blood, and then following the droplets to the other side. Her dark hair blows in the wind and she tries to calm down her breathing. "What the hell is going on?" The wind carries her words through the city.

I could say the same thing, Sam. But, why are you everywhere I need to be?

FIVE

Samara

Walking through the door of my apartment, I slip off my boots and walk through the small hallway into the kitchen. The couch is empty, so Camille must have gone to her dad's today. I walk over to my cabinet, grab a wine glass, and fix myself a drink.

The memories from today flash through my head and I shiver, trying my best to forget the ordeal. After the police arrived, everyone had to answer their fair share of questions and Francis told me she would be taking the rest of the day off. "I suggest you do the same, I'll explain everything to Mrs. Shapiro tomorrow."

I leave my glass on the counter and decide to change out of these clothes. To be fair, I have been in them since 3 a.m. I change into some sweatpants and an oversized shirt, enjoying the early day off. I don't get many of these, but under the circumstances, it isn't that relaxing. It's heartbreaking to know that two families are going to have to deal with the loss of a loved one today. We didn't get any information on the victims after the fall between the police and our half day. I can't keep getting the short end of the stick, especially now that my job is on the line.

The door opens and Camille walks through the entrance. "What are you doing home early?" Her eyes glance to the glass in my hand. "And drinking? It's the middle of the day."

I chuckle at her and pat the couch beside me. "I'm sure you want to hear all about how I had to deal with two deaths–correction, murders–today." She sits down beside me quickly and kicks off her shoes in the process.

"Tell me everything."

I shake my head and say, "You first. Did you see your dad today?"

She nods and holds my gaze. "It was good, actually." The surprise on my face must have been evident. "I was surprised too. I mean, he definitely doesn't have the best track record." I nod agreeing with her. As I take another sip, she continues. "The house had been cleaned and he shaved that stupid beard. His clothes didn't smell like alcohol. He's been sober for three weeks."

I smile and see the happiness in her eyes. "Camille, I'm so glad." She reaches in and hugs me. "Are you going to be spending more time there?" Part of me doesn't want to hear the answer. I love Camille like a little sister and sometimes even like a daughter, but I know that if she wants to spend time with her own father, that she should.

"I think maybe a couple days a week. Half the time there and half the time here. I don't want to get my hopes up."

It comforts me knowing she will still be here. "That's a good place to start. I'd be too lonely without you." She laughs and pushes me slightly.

"Now it's your turn." I tell her all about the Jane Doe death at the subway and then John Doe's death today at lunch. I make sure not to go so in depth that she throws up, but I have to give her a little gore because that's what she wants. When the topic comes up about the cuts for work, Camille's gaze becomes worrisome. "What's the plan?"

I shake my head and finish off what's left of my glass. "I'm doing the best I can now. I guess I just have to work harder."

"Don't work yourself to death, okay?"

I nod and smile as I kiss her head. "Always worried about me."

"Who else is going to take care of me?" We both chuckle and I walk over to the sink, careful to put my glass in and not break it.

"Have you done school work today?"

Camille nods and walks over to the desk she has facing the windows beside the couch. "I did a little this morning before I went to Dad's. I'm going to finish the rest now."

"Okay, I'm going to be in my room catching up on some sleep." Online school was the best option for Camille. She's too feisty for public school. Plus, this gives her more time to do what she wants to do.

I walk to my bedroom and get under the covers, the sunlight that leaks through my window has a soft glow. I look at the buildings out my window and slowly close my eyes, careful to think about the happy things instead of the gruesome deaths I dealt with today. Soon, the warmth from the sun and my blankets puts me at ease as I slip off into sleep.

It's hard to sleep when you feel like someone is watching you. The hair stands up on the back of your neck and you get chills all the way down your body.

I slowly open my eyes and they adjust to the thin beam of light that floods through the windows. After blinking a couple times, I check the clock beside my bed to see that it's midnight. Groaning, I sit up and look outside my window to see all the buildings lit up. I throw the covers off and walk to the den to see what Camille is up to.

"I shouldn't have slept that much." Camille is sitting on the couch, scrolling on her phone while the television plays in the background. I see an empty chinese takeout box on the coffee table and Camille turns to look at me.

"There's some in the fridge for you. I wasn't sure when you would wake up." Nodding, I walk over to the fridge and put the box in the microwave. "I decided to let you sleep. You had a long day and it doesn't look like it's going to get any better within the next couple weeks."

I smile and reply, "Thanks, and you got that right."

After getting my food out of the microwave, I walk over to the couch and sit down beside Camille. "I think I have an idea." She puts her phone down and proceeds to turn off the television as I cross my legs and face her. "What if I did a story about the two murders today?"

She turns her head slightly to the side and replies, "The police haven't released any information, let alone that they're related." I shake my head and put my food down on the coffee table after taking a bite. "That's the thing, though. They are related."

"How?" Camille turns to face me better and leans forward, anticipating what I'll say next.

"They're related, because they were killed in similar ways." I lean back against the couch and let the tension wash from my shoulders.

"One was sliced up and one was dropped from a building. How is that similar?"

I shake my head and hold up my hand. "I mean, they both had scratch, claw marks on them, and they were missing organs."

"Missing organs?" She takes a big breath and sits there for a moment contemplating. I nod and explain that Jane Doe was missing her eyes, while John Doe looked to be missing his heart.

"There was a hole so deep in his chest, and it was just empty. It looked like whatever the killer wanted, he got it and more."

Camille holds up her hand and interjects. "So, could it be the start of a serial killer?"

"Probably. Serial killers are usually defined as three or more, and there's been two in a day."

Camille shivers and makes a groaning noise. "Stuff like this gives me the chills."

I nod and chuckle. "I know the feeling. I woke up because I felt like someone was watching me." I wiggle my fingers towards her and start to make spooky noises. She quickly slaps my arm and scolds me.

"Don't say things like that!" I laugh and engulf her into a hug.

"Don't worry. I'll protect you." I feel her chest quickly rise and fall with the sound of her chuckles as she returns my hug.

"I know you will."

After a moment, she releases me and asks, "What do you need me to do?" Camille has connections throughout the city, mostly people who just know her. She helps me get information whenever a story comes up, it gives me an upper hand. However, I don't know if I want her involved in this one. If the suspect is actually a serial killer and they find out someone is looking into them, it could be dangerous. "For now, I just need to work on getting profiles built up for the victims. It's a good idea to see how they're related or if they have anything in common."

After saying goodnight to Camille and telling her to get some rest for her school tomorrow, I head to my room and decide to grab a notebook to start writing the facts. The first page I leave blank, it may be weird if anyone finds it and I don't want them snooping through it. Once I get to a good page, I write what I know:

- Jane Doe: mid to late twenties, scratch (claw) marks along back from base of neck to lumbar region, eyes missing
- Tech guy: face clawed, hole in chest (possible heart missing?)

I text Francis and ask her to send me all the pictures and videos that she has of the murders. She responds almost instantaneously. "It's almost like she never sleeps." The heavy silence of my room responds with creaks in the walls. I print out the pictures and take screenshots from the video of the man falling from the roof. I also use the photos of the blood that I took on the roof. "I'll have to get more information on them when I get to work tomorrow." I put up the notes and make my way to my room, rolling over thoughts in my head about that past couple hours. The only connection between the two is that they were scratched and that they each have organs missing; although, that's just a hunch for the tech guy. I could be reading too much into this, but not only could this story expose a serial killer loose in New York, but it could also guarantee my stay at Shapiro Informatics.

I worked hard to get this job and I don't plan to lose it.

SIX

Rowan

Seeing those two reporters really threw me for a loop. There's only been two murders and both times, those two have been there. It worries me. How can two humans be involved in this investigation as I am, considering that it's a supernatural creature we're dealing with. After the situation with the second victim was taken care of, I watched to see what those two would do. They simply just went home and I was relieved. Now, I can do what I need to do without them interfering, for a little while at least.

Rushing back to the hideout, I meet Rose first. "Rowan? Didn't you just leave?"

"Where's Mekaia?" She points towards the direction of his office.

"He hasn't come out since you left." I nod and walk towards his office, feeling her eyes burning a hole through my head.

"Mekaia!" I burst through the doors and he already looks annoyed.

"What is it now?"

"Another murder." Mekaia and I go to the crime scene and stay in the shadows, observing from afar. After filling him in on the situation, he calls one of the informants from the police department.

"Uriah, I need you to get as much information as possible on the two murders that happened today. Keep me in the loop." He hangs up without even hearing a response.

"What do you want me to do?"

"I want you to find whatever this is." His voice is irritated. Of course, there is a trespasser who is a serial killer in our territory. It's not exactly the best combination.

"Do whatever you have to do to figure out who this is and stop them."

"Whatever I have to do?"

He shakes his head and replies, "That's what I said, Rowan." Understanding the fact that he's already annoyed beyond measure, I simply nod and excuse myself.

Once out of earshot, I call Uriah on my own accords. "Uriah, it's Rowan."

"Hey Rowan, is this about what Mekaia just called about?" I shake my head, even though he can't see me. I look around while replying, making sure no one is within earshot. "Dealing with these two murders going on, I need you to get me information on two reporters."

"Reporters?"

I let out a deep breath, "Yes, reporters. I think they could be valuable help while being kept in the dark. Maybe they can help me find out who it is."

After giving their names to Uriah, he found them fairly quickly and some information on them. Francis Bales and Samara Allen. They both work for Shapiro Informatics, Francis is Samara's superior. Basic information comes along with this: birthday, age, how long they've lived here, and most importantly, where they live. I should pay each of their houses a visit.

Getting to Francis' place first was short, considering she lives very close to work. However, once I got to her apartment she wasn't there. I was sure that both of them had gone home instead of going back to work. It wasn't hard picking the lock, I've done it plenty of times before. Her small apartment felt cramped and her cat didn't like me too much. She had flowers and plants covering every surface available, which ended up making me sneeze the whole time.

After finding nothing at her house, I decided to move towards Samara's house. Except, she was home, sleeping. There was also a younger girl there, but I don't think they were related. She was too young to be living on her own. It didn't make sense to me. Samara's room is lined with windows that show everything in her apartment. From the building directly in front of the apartment, I can look right into her bedroom from the roof. She's sleeping soundly, wrapped in the covers while the other girl has ordered some chinese take out. I couldn't just go barging into their home with them in it.

My plan is to have an alias as a private investigator, and to team up with one of these reporters. They have eye witness accounts just like me, and because they're human, they'll be able to put their information into a different point of view than myself. Once we team up and they give me all the information they have, I will be able to find this trespasser for Mekaia, and everything will be set right.

SEVEN

Samara

The next day, more information was released to the press regarding the first death. After going to a press conference in front of the police station, along with a crowd of other reporters and journalists, we learned as much as the police would provide us with. The first victim was Jenny Harris, a twenty-four year old student at New York University. Francis and I already knew the details about her missing eyes and the location she was killed. They haven't identified the killer as a serial killer yet, but I'm sure after further investigation of the tech guy, they'll link the two together.

I write down the extra information into my booklet and begin to head to work. Since I was an eyewitness to the second murder, I already have more information on it than anyone else. I'm not sure who he was or how old he was, but his heart was definitely missing. The factors that connect these two murders are the scratches across their body and a missing organ.

"Sam!" I've made it to work and have settled into my desk, when Francis comes trotting in. "I got some information about the second murder." She's breathless and her cheeks are a rosy red, no doubt stained from the raging wind outside. She must've been in a hurry to get here and tell me.

"Well? Spill it." She pulls up a chair and ties back her unruly curly bob the best she can and holds a booklet in her lap. "Twenty-five year old Mark Nelson. He worked at the company where he was killed." I nod, waiting for her to continue with anything that is actually useful. "You were right, his heart was missing. But no one seems to understand why he would be killed."

"No one had any animosity towards him?"

Francis shakes her head and takes another breath. "Apparently he was pretty well known throughout the company and everyone liked him."

I lean back in my chair and run my hands through my long hair. "The two must be related in some way if they're the victims of a serial killer."

Francis shakes her head once again. "The only correlation is that they were both missing organs after being killed. They were completely different people."

I nod and agree with her statement, pulling out my own booklet of information. "Jenny was a student at NYU and Mark was a tech guy at a company."

Francis looks at the information I have laid out in my book, continuing my train of thought, "Different ages, different backgrounds, different jobs. Nothing alike."

The conversation dies down there and we both promise to inform each other if we hear any more theories on the murders. The day drags on afterwards but in the end it's finally time to go home. I decide to take a cab home instead of walking all the way through the brazen wind.

"Hey, how was work?" Camille is sitting at her desk with her laptop and notebooks opened. I let out a long breath as I take off my coat and put my purse down next to the couch.

"Long and tiring."

"Any leads on those murders you saw?" I shake my head as I walk over to the fridge and pull out some leftovers from the other night, popping them into the microwave.

"There's no connection at all, not a single one. Other than the missing organs but that's after the murder."

Before Camille can open her mouth to reply, stern knocks come from the door. I look at Camille and she looks slightly panicked. "Are you expecting anyone today?"

Suspicion rising in my voice, she chuckles nervously and replies, "No, not today."

I send her a smile, "I'm just picking." She smiles sheepishly and turns back to her laptop. *Not today, huh?* I think to myself. Walking to the door, still in my work clothes, I look through the peephole and see a taller man standing firmly outside the door. He looks from side to side down the hallway and then looks directly back to the door.

Before he has a chance to knock again, I open the door, careful to leave the chain connected and the door locked. "Can I help you?" His outfit is somewhere between casual and formal with a white collared dress shirt under the trenchcoat he's wearing. He stands in silence for a moment, meeting my hazel eyes with his blue ones. I look around slightly, he's still silent. I shift on my feet and clear my throat. He blinks and then looks down for a moment.

"Oh, I'm sorry. Are you Samara Allen?"

"Yes, how can I help you?" I reiterate my question and he looks back up.

"My name is Theo Beckett and I'm a private investigator." I shut the door, unhook the chain, and reopen the door to stand in the frame as he continues speaking. "My client is looking into the murder of Jenny Harris."

I perk up at the name of one of my victims and ask him, "What does this have to do with me?" His face is unreadable as he continues with his explanation.

"After further investigation, I discovered that you were at the crime scene. You did a report on it."

I nod, "Yes, I did. But, what does that have to do with your private investigation?" He fumbles through his pockets and outstretches his hand, handing me a card.

"That's my information. If you would be interested in partnering up to work through this investigation together, I'm sure it would benefit us both."

I smirk slightly at him, "I'll keep that in mind. Thank you."

"Have a good night Ms. Allen."

I close the door and lock it, watching him out of the peephole to be sure he leaves. "Who was that?" I walk back into the kitchen and Camille is turned around in her seat, looking at me questioningly.

"A private investigator who's working on the Jenny Harris murder."

"That girl who got killed?" Her question is filled with curiosity and I nod in response. "What does that have to do with you?"

I chuckle slightly, "He wants to partner up for the investigation. He saw my report on it."

Camille stands and walks closer towards me. "This could help you get more insider information. If you two work together you're going to have to talk about it, and this could lead to—" Her words are making me connect the dots faster than she can finish her sentence.

"A breakthrough in my report, and an automatic stay at Shapiro Informatics."

EIGHT

Rowan

After sitting in front of her apartment for about an hour, Samara finally walks through the building and up to her apartment. The whole day I had been preparing for this. I had Uriah make me some business cards to seem legit, and I put on clothes with some more color instead of just black. I walk through the building and make my way up to her apartment. She's barely had any time to sit down, so no doubt she'll be able to answer the door.

Once I arrive, I knock firmly on the door and wait for a response. After a few moments, I can feel her presence through the door. I raise my hand to knock again, but the door opens before I have the chance to. She doesn't open the door all the way, but what I can see of her makes a lump form in my throat.

She hasn't had any time to change out of the clothes she wore to work, and her hair is in a firm bun. Red is definitely her color, as the glossy lipstick makes her cheekbones seem higher. I must've been a statue for too long, because she clears her throat and I bring my eyes to meet hers. "Oh, I'm sorry. Are you Samara Allen?"

"Yes, how can I help you?" Her voice, soft but defiant. She definitely stands her ground.

"My name is Theo Beckett and I'm a private investigator." She closes the door and if I couldn't feel her unchaining it, I would've thought she ended the conversation there. When she opens the door wider this time, I continue talking.

"My client is looking into the murder of Jenny Harris." I can see that she pays more attention at the mention of the first victim.

"What does this have to do with me?" Definitely a smart mouth.

"After further investigation, I discovered that you were at the crime scene. You did a report on it." If I can get her to work with me, then it'll add to the sources I get. Plus, being in a human point of view may alter the way I find out what's happening.

"Yes, I did. But, what does that have to do with your private investigation?" How can she not get it? I begin to reach into my coat pocket, becoming suddenly aware that my hands have become sweaty from her deflecting. *That's never happened before*, I think to myself. Grabbing one of the cards, I hold it out to her, watching her as she takes it. The heat from her skin radiating towards mine.

"That's my information. If you would be interested in partnering up to work through this investigation together, I'm sure it would benefit us both."

After she looks at the card, she smirks slightly, keeping that intimidating aurora around her. "I'll keep that in mind. Thank you."

I nod and reply quickly, "Have a good night, Ms. Allen." She closes her door and I take my leave, beginning to walk away from her apartment. I don't go far, I just go up to the building that looks into her apartment, deciding to see what they're up to now. Samara and the younger girl who lives with her are talking in the kitchen, until Samara leaves to her room. I can see that she goes into the bathroom, probably to take a shower.

"Are you being a pervert?" I turn abruptly to meet the emerald eyes of Rose.

"What are you doing here?" She shrugs and walks over to the edge of the roof we're on, and looks towards Samara's apartment.

"Getting tired of me already?" I scoff and shake my head, looking back down to the apartment we're observing.

"I was tired of you years ago." She slaps my shoulder and pretends to be hurt.

"Don't say such mean things. I thought we had something special."

"We didn't." My answer comes quickly, almost before she can finish getting her words out. I forget how annoying she can get when she's whiny.

"Then what were all those times in your old apartment?"

"Hookups. No strings attached. I thought we both made that clear."

She chuckles at the harshness in my voice, "I'm kidding Rowan. You've been so tense lately."

Turning away from her, I look back to the apartment. Samara is back in the kitchen, but in an oversized long sleeve and shorts. Her and the younger girl are talking about something while looking at the computer. "It's this case I'm working on. Have you heard about the murders?" Rose nods and follows my gaze.

"Word spreads fast. I'm guessing that's what you and Mekaia sneak off to talk about?" I nod and she puts one of her legs against the edge and rests her elbow on her knee. "So, how does this girl fit into everything?"

I sigh and reply, "She's a reporter who happened to be at both of the murders. I figure it may help me to think in the mindset of a human and get a different opinion."

"Wait, you told her what we are?"

I shake my head and turn back to her, grabbing her elbow, "Don't you dare accuse me of such disloyalty." She gulps and the fire in her eyes diminishes slightly. It's treason to tell humans about the supernatural.

"She doesn't know and she won't. She doesn't need to." She nods as I let go of her and turn back to watch the two girls speak. "I have to go see Mekaia." I leave the edge of the roof and begin to walk towards the exit.

"Rowan," I stop in my tracks and look over my shoulder. "Please be careful." I nod and continue walking, my thoughts filled with the raven haired reporter.

NINE

Samara

"Sam, is it okay if I have a friend over while you're at work today?" I've just gotten ready and started to fix my cup of coffee when Camille sits up on the couch with her phone in hand.

"Sure, anyone I know?"

She shakes her head and replies, "Just someone from school." *School*.

"How have classes been going?" She nods and reaches for her computer, turning it on and the bright screen making her squint her eyes.

Typing away, she tells me about her classes, "I've been thinking about picking up art classes for next year." I nod my head as I walk over to the couch and sit beside her. She turns the computer towards me so I can read the information on the classes.

"That's a good idea. You've always enjoyed art."

"I'm pretty good at it too." I chuckle at her confidence and nod before I go to grab my jacket.

"Are you going to give that private investigator a call?"

I slip my jacket on and turn back to Camille. "Maybe. I think I might talk to Francis about it before I make any decisions."

"Okay, see you later." After leaving my house, I take a cab to work, just to avoid any unwanted rain due to the overcast outside. I make my way to my cubicle and pull out my notebook to see if there's any more lines I can cross. Before I get too far, Francis walks in and leans against my desk.

"Have you heard anything?"

I shake my head in defeat, "There's literally nothing to connect the dots between the two."

Francis gently nods, "I haven't picked up anything either, and no one at the station is budging."

I reach into my purse and take out the card I got from the private investigator. "A private investigator showed up at my apartment yesterday wanting to work together on the Jenny Harris case."

Francis looks towards me sharply and takes the card from my hand. "Theo Beckett, I've never heard of him."

I nod in agreement, logging onto my desktop at the same time. "Yeah but, you know how many there are in New York."

"But he just showed up to your apartment? That's creepy."

I turn my head to meet her eyes and slightly nod, "I mean, he is a private investigator. It probably didn't take much digging." I can feel Francis become uneasy.

"Are you going to get into contact with him?"

I nod and reply, "I think so. If he can help us with the investigation then there's no reason not to." She pulls out her phone and turns on her camera.

"Do you mind?" She says motioning towards the card.

"Not at all, just keep me in the loop if you find anything." She snaps the photo and hands me back the card before disappearing into the office.

The office was buzzing this morning, everyone whispering about the rumors of the cuts to our department. The elevator doors open, and I catch a glimpse of blonde hair walking through the doors. Sitting up straight in my chair, I see that it is Ms. Shapiro herself, no doubt coming to shut down rumors and give us a layout of what's going to happen. As Ms. Shapiro shuffles in, her assistant walks closely behind her holding her bags and coffee. She clears her throat and firmly says, "Everyone, pay attention."

Most of the office froze the moment she walked through the elevator, but now everyone else is as still as they can be. Those who can't see stand up from their chairs, and everyone listens intently.

"I know there have been rumors going around about possible cuts to this specific department." I feel the room shift into worry as everyone around me holds their breath. "I'm here to tell you these aren't rumors. Starting immediately, no job here is promised." Many of the employees look down and shift on their feet, while others let out the breaths they had been holding. I sit up straighter and keep my mind focused on what she's saying. "My late husband hired too many people for this specific department, and not enough people for others." I knew this. Francis always made it known that other departments, like the photographers, didn't have enough employees and could barely keep their heads above water. "Because of this, I have to make cuts to this department, before I can start hiring for others." I see movement in my left field of vision, and I see Joshua, looking very worried. He's no doubt afraid, just like the rest of us. However, I know he's going to torture me about it, and act like he automatically has a spot.

"Eliminations will be every week, with five to ten people leaving each week." She takes a deep breath, and actually starts to look at all the employees, her eyes settle on me for what feels like forever, before she moves onto the next person. "I am truly sorry. It has been wonderful to have you all here, and if you need a reference, you have my contact information." With that, she turns sharply and walks back to the elevator, her assistant shuffling behind her. Once the doors to the elevator close, the floor is silent as everyone gathers their thoughts. The phone's start to ring and we are back to work.

Joshua makes his way over to my cubicle, I continue typing what seems like nonsense on my computer. "Hey." I glance up at him, the same worried face is still there but it's replaced with something else, nervousness? "What can I help you with?" The words fly out my mouth as my typing gets faster.

"Well, I know we've always been on each other's bad sides and got off on the wrong-"

"Seriously?" I scoff and don't even bother to make eye contact with him. "You have been nothing but an insufferable prick who thinks he is above every-"

"Go out with me."

My typing ceases immediately, my whole body feels like it stings. Glancing up at him, his face is a couple shades whiter, if he wasn't nervous before, my silence is definitely sealing the deal. "Sam?" Joshua's voice snaps me out of whatever trance I was in to meet his eyes.

"What?"

He chuckles slightly, "Go out with me. On a date." My mouth hangs open, the repeated words making their way into my brain. "You know, two people alone, eating dinner, chatting about life?"

"I know what a date is, Joshua." He smiles, the nervousness seems to fade with our normal bickering intertwining in this serious moment.

"Then go on one with me." I roll my lips together and shake my head, sighing quietly.

"Why do you want to go on a date with me?"

"I think you're beautiful." His words only slightly take me back. I know that I'm good looking but being called beautiful by someone who I thought hated my guts feels more solid than being looked at in a bar. "You're a spitfire who knows how to shut me up. Not many people can do that, and I'd like to experience it more." He winks at me and my cheeks flush red. Turning my head away from his gaze, I shake the blush away. I close my eyes briefly and take a deep breath. He clears his throat once and my eyes open but they don't return to him. "Way to leave a guy waiting."

The sticky notes that sit on my desk separate as I grab one. "What are you-"

"Tomorrow night, Pang Chao Takeout. Your place, not mine. Have ice cream in your freezer, and a good bottle of riesling." I hand him the sticky note with my number, the order for takeout, and a time. He takes the note and smiles kindly, something I'm not used to seeing from him.

He nods but responds quickly, "Bossy. I like it. See you then, Sunshine."

When he walks away, I watch him for a moment before I pick back up on what I was working on, until my phone starts to ring. "Samara Allen spe-"

"Sam!" Pulling the phone back slightly from my ear, I hear Francis speaking on the other end.

"You know, you should really use your inside voice."

"There's been another murder."

TEN

Rowan

I haven't been able to find Mekaia since my conversation with the reporter. He's not in his usual hangout spots and Rose and Uriah haven't heard anything from him. Apparently he hasn't been heard from since the day before yesterday. I've tried calling him, but no answer and even his apartment has been abandoned. I need to give him an update on the reporter. I should be expecting a call from her soon.

After coming to an end in my search for Mekaia at his office, my phone begins to ring. My brain hopes for an answer from the reporter so we can get the show on the road, but I'm left disappointed as Uriah's voice sounds from the other side of the phone. "Have you found Mekaia?" The annoyed tone present in my voice makes itself known.

"No, but I did find three bodies the police just pulled out of the river." Uriah works as our mole at the police station, and he proves to be an effective one.

"On my way." I respond quickly and make my way to the police station, meeting him there.

Uriah lets me in through the back and walks me down to the morgue. When the doors open, I see three bodies laid on the metal tables, covered with a white sheet, only their faces showing. There are two men and one female. "What's the cause of death?"

Uriah walks to the opposite side of the room as he speaks, "The two males died from drowning and the female died from a gunshot wound to the abdomen."

I shake my head and scoff, "What does this have to do with the murders that I'm looking into? My murders are supernatural, these are just normal New York crime junkies."

Uriah responds quickly with, "Yeah but do normal New York crime junkies end up with missing organs?"

He begins to walk over to the male on the far side. He's a dark skinned gentleman who looks to be in his older thirties. "Both the drowning victims' time of death were around the same time. We've identified this one as Shaolic McCray." Uriah moves to the next table, where the other male lays and continues, "This is Howard Anderson. Both of them work at the docks together."

"Okay, who was missing what?" I'm getting more impatient as the time drags on. For all I know, another murder could be happening right now. Uriah sighs, annoyed at me no doubt.

"Shaolic was missing his liver, Howard his intestines, and Lily," he motions towards the woman on the last table, "she was missing her lungs."

"How exactly did they die from drowning and getting shot before they died from getting their organs taken?" Uriah walks over to the edge of the room where the computer and papers sit. He comes back and hands me a folder of papers.

"They were killed before their organs were taken."

I thank Uriah and take some pictures of the victims and their wounds. No matter how gruesome the reporter would think they are, she needs to see them. My phone rings again and this time it's Mekaia. "Where the hell have you been?"

"Rowan, I don't need a sermon from you right now." He sounds tired and out of breath, like he's about to pass out.

"Where are you?" By now, I'm outside the back of the police station, the hair on my neck stands up waiting for his reply. I hear shuffling and then a sudden drop.

"Mekaia!" Rose's voice comes through the phone quietly and I know he's at his office. As fast and sneaky as I can, I let my wings rip out my shirt and take me to him. With him being my oldest friend and closest confidant, worry fills my chest at hearing him collapse.

Once I arrive at his office, Rose has him sitting up against the wall, a water bottle in her hand. "What happened?" Mekaia looks up, his green eyes look lifeless as he groans.

"I told Rose I'm fine." I look up to meet Rose for a glance, and toss her a nod to the other side of the room. She leaves the bottle in his hand and makes sure he's in a good spot before she withdraws her support.

"Rowan,"

"What happened?"

She sighs and looks back over to Mekaia, he sips his water slowly. "I don't know. He came in and he looked exhausted, not much worse than he does right now." I make a move to go back over to him but Rose grabs my forearm. I look up and her eyes are worried, her red hair falls around her face. "Rowan, when he came in his eyes were red. I've never seen him like that before in all the time I've been here."

I inhale a slow breath and look down at my feet. This has been happening more frequently, and everytime I show concern he shuts me down. "Thanks, Rose. I'll take care of it now."

"But Rowan-"

"I said, I'll take care of it." Her mouth forms into a straight line, and she lowers her gaze from mine.

I walk over to Mekaia and sling his arm over my shoulder. I push his office doors open and help him sit in his chair. After closing the door and making sure he's still breathing from across the room, I tell him what we've found out, "Three more bodies showed up. I'm waiting for the reporter to get in touch with me."

"Three more? Damn, it seems like they're speeding up." Mekaia sips the last of his water and throws the bottle somewhere beside him. "They have an agenda. I want you to figure out what it is." I nod and turn to exit. "Rowan," I look back over my shoulder and one of his eyes is red again. My heart races, but I try to stay calm. "Figure this out. Now." His words are firm and they hold a certain amount of threat. My dominant side thrashes in my body, but I force a simple nod and exit.

On the way out, Rose shoots me a sympathetic glance, and it looks like she wants to apologize. I keep walking. My thoughts are cloudy with so many scenarios of today and possible scenarios which could happen. Busy with my thoughts, I almost miss my phone ringing. It's an unknown number, but I answer anyway. "Hello?"

"Mr. Beckett?"

The reporter, she called. "This is he." My voice switches to a professional manner and the reporter continues talking.

"This is Samara Allen, the reporter you gave your card to?"

"Yes, Ms. Allen. How can I help you?"

"I'd like to take you up on your offer. How about we meet?"

ELEVEN

Samara

Mr. Beckett and I decided to meet up at a cafe near the murder location that Francis and I saw. The late Saturday morning weather was muggy with low hanging fog and a strong breeze. By the time I order and sit near the windows, the rain starts. Not long after, Mr. Beckett walks in. The water from his umbrella makes a small puddle on the floor and he wipes his shoes on the welcome mat. As he begins to look around, I gently raise my hand, signaling him over. He stalks over and takes off his trenchcoat, showing a black long sleeve underneath. "I wasn't sure what you liked, so I just got you a black coffee." I motioned towards the white mug sitting in front of him.

"Thank you." He sips the coffee and scrunches his nose slightly before grabbing some sugar packets on the table.

"Where should we begin?" He stirs his coffee and I pull out my notebook to explain what I know. "We already know that all the victims have been missing organs, so the only lead that I could possibly have would be the black market." I flip to the page with the pictures of the murders that Francis sent me.

His eyes reach mine and a small smirk appears on his lips. "Aren't these classified?"

I nod once and respond, "Technically, yes. Except these were taken before the police got there." I hand them over to him so he can get a closer look and he hands me a file in return.

"Three more murders at the docks this week. All found on the same day."

I open the folder and cringe, "Aren't these classified?" I slightly smirk as they're coming from a literal police file. "You could've given me a warning."

His facade seems to fade as the smile slowly drops. "This investigation isn't easy or polite. It's gruesome. These are deaths of people who have been ripped open, and it's only going to get worse if we don't figure this out."

I turn my head to the side and give him a stern look. "You think I don't know that? I saw this girl," I point to the picture of Jenny, the first murder, "With her eyes cleaned out of her sockets. Don't tell me something I already know." The eye contact for the next couple seconds is intense, but it passes when he looks back down to the pictures.

"All different people, all different organs." He continues to flip through the pictures as I look through the file. These poor people, living their normal lives just to have their whole future taken away from them.

"It's like they're building their own person." An intake of breath makes me look up.

"What did you just say?" His mouth hangs ajar just a little as he stares at me.

"What?"

He repeats his question, "I asked you, what did you just say?" His voice becomes darker and his patience wears thin.

"I said that it looks like someone is trying to make their own person. Building their own human."

He grabs the file from my hands and puts my pictures beside his. "I mean, they seem to be going after different organs in the different murders. There haven't been any repeats of organs that we know of. Depending on who you're talking to, the number of organs in the human body differ, but generally there are seventy eight." I stir my coffee and wait for his response. I understand how far fetched it sounds, but it's all I can come up with.

He looks back up at me, "Aren't you a reporter?"

I chuckle and nod, "Yes, but I still went to college. Anatomy, you know, that science class people take."

He doesn't laugh or even give me a small smile, instead he huffs out a breath and switches his gaze between the several pictures. "So you're telling me that there's going to be a total of seventy eight murders?"

I shake my head, "Not if this psycho starts to double up. They have an agenda, they're speeding up their kills, planning something."

I take a sip of my drink and look towards his face. He's pale and he seems sweaty. "What aren't you telling me?"

"I don't want you working this case anymore. It was my mistake in trying to get you involved, so stay out of it." I scoff and shake my head as he puts my pictures into the file and reaches for my notebook. I grab his wrist before he gets to it and I can tell this surprises him.

"You don't know me. You got me involved and I know just as much as you do, so don't think you can just come and take my part of the investigation and take it as your own. That's not how this is going to work."

My grip on his wrist becomes tighter but he still manages to turn his arm free. "Fine." He finally says, "If you want to continue on this investigation, you know, the one with everyone dying, then go right ahead. I'm not going to be responsible for you."

"I don't expect you to be." I grab the file from his hand and retake my pictures. "You have my contact information, when you're actually ready to start explaining what you know and stop treating me like a fragile child, then maybe we can get somewhere." I stand to leave and walk straight out of the cafe. The rain has subsided for now, so when I exit the cafe I walk straight to the road and call a taxi. I watch his figure fade from my view as the taxi speeds off in the direction of my apartment.

"Sam, you're home so soon?" I walk into my kitchen to see Camille sitting on the couch, computer in her lap.

"Let's just say Mr. Beckett isn't ready to have a partner in this investigation."

"Well, tell me what happened!" I take off my shoes and jacket as she slides over to make room on the couch for me, by now the rain is back and I watch as the clouds hang low around the buildings near mine.

"He told me that he didn't want to feel responsible for me during this investigation. He also tried to take my pictures and notebook, but I wouldn't let him."

"Have there been more murders?"

I nod and kick my feet up on the coffee table, careful not to spill her drink. "Three more on his end. Whoever is doing this is picking up their pace." I catch her worried gaze as I look out to the building directly in front of us, any one of those people could be next. "What is it, Camille?" I turn to face her and she shakes her head.

"I think I agree with Mr. Beckett. I don't want you doing this anymore."

"Are you-"

"Yes I am serious Sam." She interrupts me and lets out a sigh, "You're basically all I have left. If whoever is doing this hears about you investigating, what if they turn their attention to you? I can't have you getting hurt."

I smile softly,wrap an arm around her shoulders, and kiss her forehead. "I promise that nothing is going to happen to me, and I'm definitely not going to let anything happen to you, either." I hold out my pinky finger to her, and she wraps hers around mine. "Promise."

"Promise." We kiss our hands and Camille unwraps her arms around me.

"Hey, before I forget, guess what happened to me today?" Camille grabs her computer and opens it to begin some school work, but she's still listening by the head tilt towards me. "I got asked out on a date." Her computer flies off her lap as she squeals and moves closer to me.

"No freaking way!"

I flinch with her loud voice. "What is it with everyone not using their inside voices?" She moves back closer to me and I tell her about Joshua asking me out today at work.

"So badass!" I give her a pointed look for the language. Just because I'm grown and have a foul mouth, doesn't mean she has to. "He is so insufferable but he likes you! Oh my god, it's like an enemies to lovers trope!"

I hold up my hands in defeat, "Hold on, it's just a date. No one said anything about us being lovers."

She chuckles and shakes her head, "Come on Sam, how long has it been since you let loose and had a good time?" She wiggles her eyebrows a little bit, "If you know what I'm saying."

I roll my eyes and shake my head, "We are done with this conversation." We both laugh and Camille snuggles into my arms. We then sit there, enjoying the sound of the rain coming down and the view of the lights beginning to turn on in some buildings.

TWELVE

Rowan

It's like they're building their own person. The reporter's voice repeats in my head over and over again. To a human, it seems like a feeble joke on their end to try and make sense of it. To us, the supernatural, it's far from it. We believe in all the folklore, all the scary stories you tell your kids, we are them. They are the stories of our lives throughout the centuries, and what she said struck a chord with me from folklore of my own lineage.

When the fallen are cast out of heaven, it seems hopeless to try and get back in. While many don't want to, like me, others dread the human world and its antics. Some want to go home. Piece by piece and day by day, our supernatural abilities fight back against us, and ultimately end us. The longer our stay away from our true home in Heaven, the shorter our lives are. In

Heaven we are infinite servers of God, but on earth, basically in Hell, we are anything but infinite. Mekaia has been here the longest, probably since the world truly started, and I think it has slowly built up and is now taking its toll. The separation from our home causes several kinds of emotional, mental and physical issues; enough to kill us, immortality and all. There is a story, and it's called a story because no one actually thinks it's real, but it's in some of our relics from the previous centuries.

A perfect sacrifice, mind, body and soul, can get you back into Heaven. However, that's pretty vague and can literally mean a million different things. Many people have tried throughout the years to test this theory and eliminate possible answers: innocent children, baby animals, themselves. Nothing availed after these sacrifices. The fallen angel eventually succumbed to the effects of their situation, and slowly descended into madness and death. Sometimes I sit and wonder, when will my time come? Will I go quickly, or will the madness slowly eat away at me? It's been over five hundred years since I've been on earth, and every year the possibility of dying gets closer and closer. God sits up in the sky along with his archangels and laughs at me, at us. Mekaia is showing the first real signs of the end: his red eyes, the absence in his presence, the lack of energy in his being. It hurts knowing that he is possibly nearing the end, he is a great leader, and my first friend.

I've been sitting in this secured section of the library that is for just the supernatural, staring at pages that I've been reading and rereading. Nothing is helping me, or even pointing me in the right direction. But knowing that this killer is supernatural, and now Samara showing me the perspective of them possibly being a fallen, like me? The sacrifices before were clean, easy, simple. These killings are the work of a monster, who will stop at nothing to get what they want. We can be ruthless and vulgar given any opportunity. It's literally our job to cause destruction and harm, to keep the balance of good and evil, but this is way above my paygrade.

My phone ringing and someone near me shushing me drew me back to reality. My phone reads, "Reporter" and I know it's Samara calling once again.

Rolling my eyes, I answer the phone, annoyed, "What?"

"Is that any way to talk to your partner?"

The word partner would make it seem I care about you, I think to myself. "Don't call yourself that."

"Whatever, look. I got into a contact of mine who knows someone-"

Stopping her in the middle of her sentence, I try to finish it for her, "Let me guess, who knows someone who knows someone who knows-"

"Yes, but that's beside the point!" I hear her huff and decide to let her finish. "They are a reliable source, and they said there are murders that aren't being investigated."

I stand still for a second before shaking my head and running my free hand across my face. "Where are we meeting?

An hour later, I'm standing outside her apartment. My hands are in my pockets and the lump in my throat grows. *I'm not going in there, am I?* I knock on the door, once, twice and before my fist hits the third time, the door swings open and I come face to face with the roommate. A dark skinned girl who looks extremely young to be living this kind of lifestyle as a roommate. "Sam!" Her voice startles me, and she smirks. "P.I is here." She blocks the entrance, making sure I won't step foot in without the reporters permission. Samara comes into my view from around the backside of the roommate.

"Camille, play nice." The girl, Camillie, glares at me but moves so Samara can get out of her apartment. She sees my confusion and says, "Oh, you didn't think we were going inside, did you?"

I clear my throat and shake my head, "Let's go."

We walk in silence down back alleyways filled with garbage and sleeping homeless people. Samara takes it in stride, not even batting an eye to our current situation. "How are you so comfortable right now?" It's not a problem for me, but I figured a priss like her would be tip-toeing around everything.

"I grew up on a farm so the dirtiness doesn't bother me, and I'm on a mission to figure this out." Farm girl, huh. I would've never guessed.

"So, what's this guy doing anyways?" She makes another turn and I follow right behind her.

"He's the door keeper for the black market auctions people have. As bad as it is, it's our first real lead."

"And you just happen to know someone from the black market?" I chuckle slightly and shake my head while she turns to glare at me.

"Camille has more connections than I ever could. She knows someone who is drinking buddies with this guy."

"The kid?" She nods. "She was in and out of the streets when she found me. She's like my secret weapon when it comes to getting better reports."

"She found you?" She nods as we get to an entrance to what looks like a bar. "Long story, but she probably saved my life." It seems like this girl, Camille, and this reporter have a good relationship. Not sure how long they have been together, but I can tell they care for each other. "We're here."

She pushes through the door and we end up inside this run down bar that smells of cigarette smoke and piss. The walls are covered in old, dusty black and gold pictures while the emerald green walls look stained. The bar is set up like a train ticket station in old London. The name across the top reads "London Station." Original. There's only a couple occupants paired with one bartender on site. Samara takes the lead, of course, and walks up to one of the men sitting alone at the bar. Even though she is normally defiant and strong willed, I can tell she's nervous by her body language. "Excuse me." She taps the man on his shoulder and he turns to face us.

"What do you want?" She tenses, no doubt the smell of his breath taking her back.

"I just had a quick question for you-"

"Go on then." Not too friendly–whether that's with the alcohol in his system, or just his personality–that much is evident.

"Do you happen to know anyone here named Jeckel?" His eyes widen and before Samara would have time to blink, he throws his beer at her and tries to bolt out the door we came through. I grab him as he tries to pass me and lead- more like drag-him out into the alleyway. "

Who the hell are you people?" His words are strained as he fights back against me. I shove him against the cold, concrete wall and shove my forearm under his throat.

"That was no way to treat a lady. Let's have a chat."

THIRTEEN

Samara

Great, now I smell like booze. Theo will not let me live this down, and I definitely don't want to think about what Camille would have to say. I go back out the door we came through and see Theo holding him up with his forearm underneath his neck, probably stopping his breathing with how red this man's face is. "I'm telling you, I don't know anything!"

"That's obviously not the case with my blouse you just ruined with your cheap beer." Theo turns his head to me and the man follows his gaze.

"I have a deal with the cops, I don't say anything out of pocket, they leave me alone!" Walking closer towards them, but still staying behind Theo because at this point, this man is unpredictable.

"Good thing we aren't the cops then." Theo fills in that blank for me. Jeckel relaxes, as much as he can with Theo's arm at his neck.

"I'll tell you whatever you want," he says between breaths, "please, just let me down!" Theo gazes back at him, seemingly waiting for my permission. I nod and he drops him. Jeckel falls to the ground, huffing and taking a moment to catch his breath.

"You owe me a blouse."

He chuckles and looks back at me, "How about a beer?"

Back inside the bar, we choose a booth away from everyone, with pretty cheap lighting, and order three drafts. I've never been one for beer, but if this is all I get out of my ruined shirt, along with some answers, I'll take it. "Jeckel is just a cover name I use for my job."

"At the black market?" He nods, we may be getting somewhere. "I've been told from a source that you were a witness in murders that aren't being investigated by the police." He nods and takes a sip, more like a chug, of his beer.

"It was about two months ago, and it looked like a massacre. Blood, skin and guts everywhere. It looked like something actually tore them apart." My imagination isn't my friend in this scenario, thinking about blood and flesh covered walls. "I called the police and they only sent one detective down."

"Who was it?" I reach inside my jacket for my notepad and begin taking notes.

"His name was Uriah. He told me if I kept quiet about this situation that they would leave my job alone." Theo tenses and rolls his shoulders back, but I don't bother looking at him. Instead, I write the name down and put a question mark beside it. "I don't know much more about it other than that. There have been rumors, whispers if you will, that something has been messing with our performance directions."

"Performance directions?" Theo finally speaks and Jeckel nods.

"Think of it like our order of things. Certain things are more popular than others, and certain things sell better. But after those murders, our big boss put an advance on these items."

"What items?" I know the answer, and don't want to hear it, but I know the only way to get to the bottom of this is to get the raw, unedited facts.

"People." I cringe and finally take a sip of my beer. Theo hasn't touched his glass this whole time and Jeckel has slowly, but surely, almost downed his entire glass. "This is the one part of my job I don't find joy in. I have a family, a little girl. We all have mouths to feed so we put the bad parts on the back burner and hope for a better outcome. Even though we know that's probably not how it will go." People. Human trafficking. It happens everywhere but just knowing

I'm actually this close to it makes me sick. I'd rather be tone deaf towards it.

"Why are they putting an advance on people if there were so many slaughtered that night?"

Jeckel shakes his head, "There is a new buyer in town. Not sure what he's looking for, but whenever we get a new shipment, the boss calls him and he comes to buy almost everyone we have. But, there's something else."

"What?" Theo speaks up again, and Jeckel starts to lean forward, and whispers his reply quietly, "I think it's the same person who killed everyone else that night."

I continuously write on my notepad, "Why?"

"The room, where they're bought. After the purchase, everyone on my side of the team gets out, locks the doors and tries to forget the sounds they hear. I can never hear them because I'm usually in another sector."

This time, Theo speaks first. "Sounds?"

He nods, "The screams of those people inside, who have just been bought, and the sounds the buyer makes."

"What does he sound like?"

Jeckel finishes off his beer and makes a face like he's trying to hold it down. "He sounds like a monster. Growling and screaming and saying something along the lines of, 'You aren't what I need!' Like he's looking for something."

I've heard enough by this point and want to start making my way back towards home. I thank Jeckel and make Theo get out of the way so I can get out of this booth and this bar. It's hard to breathe. I open the door and stand out in the alleyway. The night air is cold and feels good on my face and refreshes my throat. "Are you okay?" Theo's voice comes behind me. I turn around and face him. The moonlight reflects on his face and his black hair shines. I've never really noticed it before, but he's handsome. Right now, though, he seems concerned.

"Fine, just smell like beer and feel sick to my stomach."

He chuckles slightly as he walks closer. "Probably wasn't the best idea to drink that." I smile slightly and he takes off his jacket, leaving only a sweatshirt.

"Take off your blouse."

I stare at him and scoff which is followed by me shaking my head. "Excuse me?"

He hands me his jacket. "Take off your smelly blouse and put this on." He turns around to avert his eyes and I chuckle slightly. "Hold out your arm." He tilts his head, but does as he's told. I hang my jacket on his arm, my beer stained blouse following behind it. The cold air hits my torso and I shiver, quickly putting on his jacket and buttoning it up. I examine it before I tell him to turn around, just in case there are any openings that can be seen through.

He hands me my jacket back and keeps holding onto my blouse. He looks at his jacket and gulps before saying, "Let's get you back to your apartment." The walk was silent, but comfortable. It doesn't take us long to get back to my apartment. Once I unlock the door and look inside, I see that Camille isn't here.

Theo stands at the entry way as I walk in and turn around, leaning against the door. "I would invite you in for a drink but I think we've had too much already."

"I didn't even touch my beer." he replies nonchalantly.

I chuckle and smile slightly. "I will wash your jacket and retur-"

"Keep it. It looks better on you anyways." I nod and decide it's time to get some rest, or have a breakthrough in this case.

"Goodnight, Theo. I'll talk to you soon."

"Goodnight, Samara."

FOURTEEN

Rowan

She says the stupid name I gave her, and it sounds natural rolling off her tongue. It's not mine. *I wonder how mine would sound.* I shake my head just for another thought to fill it: *the way I could feel her warmth in that alleyway when she was changing into my jacket.* I want her to keep it, to wear it, and show it to everyone. *That's mine.* She feels familiar to me, like her existence has always been there in the back of my mind. I fly up to the building that overlooks her apartment, and watch her make her way through, straightening it up until she goes into the bathroom and out my line of sight.

My phone ringing snaps me back into reality, it's Rose. "What?"

"I think someone is onto you." Her voice reflects her worrying and, even though she can't see me, I'm visibly confused.

"What are you talking about?" I hear her sigh and shuffle on the other side of the phone.

"I'm in our library right now, it's been trashed. Most of our history books are destroyed."

I take a sharp inhale before replying, "I'm on the way." I take one last glance into her apartment and decide, that's enough for tonight.

Spreading my wings, I take off through the night sky, straight for our library. It's trashed, just like Rose said. "It's been a pain in my ass trying to clean this up." Books are everywhere, pages ripped out, stone plaques smashed into pieces. Anger boils inside me. I may not have chosen this as my destiny, it may have been forced upon me, but this was still my history. History that I lived through, history that I made.

"Do we have any idea who or what could've done this?" Rose shakes her head and picks up another book as she flipped through the intact pages.

"The security cameras of the library caught a black blurb.It happened fast and the alarm never tripped."

"So they're supernatural." She nods sadly as she continues to clean up.

"Here, I'll finish this. Will you do me a favor?" She nods as she hands me the book in her hands. "Will you get me a list of all supernatural creatures who have had clearance in the library, or who have passed through the city in the past two months?" She nods as a tear falls down her cheek. I reach up to wipe it with my thumb and cup her face. We stare at each other for what is just a moment, but she takes that moment to lean in and put her lips to mine. I pull back immediately and I see the tears come back into her eyes.

"*Rowan*, please." My name on her lips makes me cringe. She is beautiful, and we used to have a fling. But that's all it was, until she wanted more. After I found out my reason for getting kicked out of Heaven, I swore off all love. Hook ups are fine, but if they're anything like Rose, they're going to want something more; something I can't offer.

"Rose, I can't. You know that." The rejection in her eyes doesn't go unnoticed, so I add to the conversation. "You're beautiful, and you know that too." She nods and blinks away the tears.

"I'll get you those files." She walks past without saying anything more. Whenever her red hair is out of my sight, I start cleaning, and fast. I have things to do and people to see.

It takes me maybe an hour to clean before it's enough for the janitors to handle before the library opens. The sun is slowly starting to peak out beyond the city horizon. I take my phone out of my pocket and dial Mekaia. "Dude, it's too early."

"We need to talk." My stern voice shuts him up and it doesn't take me long to show up at his office. "I have news." He is sitting at his desk, twirling an envelope opener through his fingers.

"Do tell." His words don't sound friendly and I decide that he's in a mood. Hopefully what I have to say will fix that.

"I have a lead. Many connecting events with, who I believe, are the same perpetrator." He stands from his desk, still holding the opener in his hand and begins to pace around the cab.

"Multiple crimes, same guy. How does this give you a lead?"

"Because he's one of us." He visibly tenses. It's hard for a leader to hear that under his watch these crimes are going unpunished. "Our historical relics were destroyed at the library literally hours ago. I also spoke with an eye witness who is involved in the black market trades. He says there's a buyer who is purchasing people, and killing them in inhumane ways."

"Stop." His hands are white from how hard it's gripping the opener.

"What do you mean? This is clearly a lead. I just need a little help-"

"HELP?" His voice roars through the cab and I take a step back. He seems like he's going off the deep end.

"You have never needed help for anything! Suddenly we have a serial killer and you can't get your shit together long enough to find any better leads?"

I shake my head, "Mekaia, this is good news."

"Good news would be that you found the guy. Not that you have a half-assed lead." I throw my hands up and start pacing with him. "Do you know how many supernaturals we have in New York or surrounding cities? Thousands, if not millions! Do better!"

"I'm doing my best!" He turns and throws the envelope opener towards me, it catches my cheek before it lands in the cab wall behind me.

"Your best isn't good enough. I can't have my people thinking I am weak. I am their leader! Get it together." I feel the blood drip down my cheek before I wipe it away with my hand. "Get out while you're ahead."

Without saying anything, I turn and leave, slamming the door shut behind me. Rose gasps as I walk past her and out. Uriah passes by me as I'm walking out, a quick glance and a question of, "Are you alright?" To which I ignore and keep walking. In the years that I have been on Earth, and been with Mekaia, never has he actually drawn blood. He is holding on by a thread, the way he is treating everyone and his health is seemingly declining. He is a leader, and he cannot have people seeing him like this. I'm surprised he hasn't lost it on Rose or Uriah yet. I can only take so much disrespect.

My dominant side rears its head. I may not know much of anything about my life in Heaven, but I know I held true power there. I'm a skilled fighter, and even more skilled in the politics of our world. I've helped

Mekaia all the centuries I've been here. Never truly feeling content with the leadership. He's a great leader, but sometimes I wonder to myself if there's a chance I could do better. An unlucky wall meets my fist as I plow through it, breaking it to shreds.

The anger in me subsided, my mind slipping back to the reporter. Samara. I can imagine her trying to calm me down. Her fiery attitude coming to play, telling me to get it together and quit being such a drama queen. If I want something I have to take it. Knowing good and well it's probably the worst idea I've ever had, I let my wings rip out of my clothes and hoist me up into the air. Flying as fast as I can go, and as sneaky as I can be with eight foot long wings, I do everything I can in my power to get Rose, Uriah, Mekaia and Samara out of my head. Though I try my best, all but one leaves my mind.

FIFTEEN

Samara

After I shut the door, the images in my mind slowly start to dissipate. Knowing that there is a killer out there makes me sick. What if Camille is right? What if they figure out that I am trying to crack the case and write my breakthrough story? What if they decide to make me their next target?

Knowing that myself, Camille, Francis, or even Theo could be in danger makes my stomach churn. I take off my shoes and walk through the apartment folding blankets, straightening pillows, and putting glasses into the sink before I make my way to my room. Once I'm inside my bathroom, I shut the door and lean against it. Grabbing the ends of Theo's jacket, I pull it closer around me, the tightness comforting the scary thoughts away. The smell of pine leaves and vanilla surface from the underlayer of the jacket, and

I decide I don't want to take it off. But the thought of leaving beer stained skin, uncleaned, is worse.

Layer by layer, I take off my clothes and throw them into the hamper that sits in the corner. The hot water beads fall down my skin and slowly wash away layers of grime and dirt. The warmth doesn't compare to putting on Theo's jacket. His mannerisms and the way he talks seem familiar. It's like a weird sense of deja vu. Once out of the shower and in some comfortable clothes, I go to sit on the couch and turn on the TV. The background noise and light from the TV make me comfortable in the darkness as I pull out my notebook and start looking over my notes. 'Uriah' was the name Jeckel gave us, saying that he works for the police, but that he is hiding what really goes on in the black market. I also jotted down a summary of the gruesome details of the murders and the phrase Jeckel told us: "You aren't what I need."

From what I've seen, I'm assuming this is a serial killer who may be obsessed with dolls. It sounds too far-fetched, but with the assumption that the killer is stealing body parts, and the fact that I've already made the connection to them wanting to build a person, their comment strikes me as obsessive. It seems they want to build a specific type of doll, but what's the end game? Build a person with organs and then what? Do they auction it off through the black market? Do they put it up for show somewhere in the city? The questions of how, why and when rack my brain, but also, the who. Who could possibly murder people in this way? Gruesome and barbaric, and I haven't even seen the real damage apparently.

These clues alone won't help me. I don't have connections in the police department and Jeckel was Camille's lead. *Camille.* She isn't here, she had updated me that she was going to her dad's for the night. Apparently he had been doing better and she wanted to keep seeing growth. It's late and even though I want to check in on her, I let her have her space with her father. I may not like him for the things he's done, but if she's happy that he's trying, that's all that matters. Once I turn off the television, I head to my room, wrapping up in the blankets and imagining the comforting warmth of Theo's jacket.

Waking up to the sun rays leaking through my windows, I check my phone to see texts from Camille, telling me that she will be by to help me pick out an outfit for my date tonight, but she will be spending the day with her dad. Pain pings in my chest. I'm happy that they are getting along, but I can't say I don't miss her presence here.

I get ready for work quickly. Today is the one day that nothing happens, which is rare. It seems like the quiet before the storm, and I want to reject every second of it. Joshua and I glance at each other throughout the day, but don't talk. We are both probably nervous about tonight. Francis frightens me as she pops her head above the wall of my cubicle. "A little birdy told me that you have a date tonight." I roll my eyes but can't help the blush that forms on my cheeks. "Oh my god, you are excited about this."

"I wouldn't have said yes if I didn't want to go."

Francis rolls her eyes and shakes her head, "I know you might want to go but you actually seem to enjoy the idea of going on a date with *Joshua*." She says his name like poison on her tongue. I shake my head and wave her off as the work day comes to an end. In the elevator down to the parking garage, Joshua and I end up beside one another. His hand grazes my lower back and then pulls me slightly closer to him. He is taller than me, but not by much, not like Theo who towers above my frame.

"I'll see you in a couple hours."

I smile to myself and make my way home. Once I reach the entrance to my apartment, I get the feeling again that I'm being watched. This feeling has increased since the murders started, but I'm pretty sure it's just the paranoia of a serial killer lurking around. Once I open the door, Camille is in the den with different outfits laid out. She squeals when I walk inside and asks me, "Are you ready?" I sigh, seeing how excited she is for me.

"I guess this can't be a pair of shorts and a sweatshirt kind of night?"

She deadpans and shakes her head, walking towards me and grabbing my hands, "Absolutely not.

When I'm done, Joshua won't be able to keep his hands off you." God help me.

Camille fixes me up in a pair of tight fitting jeans along with some wedges and a red blouse. My raven hair has been done in curls. I rarely wear it down in front of anyone from work and Camille insisted on it. "Alright, go so you won't be late. Here's your purse, I put some surprises in there for you." Camille winks as I open my purse and see a box of condoms.

"Camille Wright! Where on earth did you get these?"

She runs as I try to grab her, "May or may not have borrowed them from the drugstore. Go, have fun, be safe!" Her voice echoes as I open the door and close it behind me. I shake my head and turn to hit a hard body.

Theo's hands reach out to grab me before I fall backwards. I grab his elbows to steady myself in these heels. Once steadied, he looks me up and down and suddenly I feel very overdressed for a casual evening. "Where are you going?" His tone is hard but his eyes say something different. I remove my hands and move his arms from my body, the warmth leaving with them.

"None of your business."

He tilts his head, "Just asking."

"I'm going to be late, whatever this is, it can wait." He doesn't protest as I walk right by him and to the elevator, but he stands still as the door closes, burning a hole through me with his blue eyes.

The cab ride to Joshua's was short and simple. Walking up, I reach for my phone and go into our text thread to tell him I was on the way up. The door to his apartment opens and there are candles everywhere, along with our takeout boxes and a tall glass of wine. My face breaks out into a huge smile as he grabs my hand and leads me inside. "You look breathtaking." A blush returns to my cheeks and I thank him as he takes me to his couch. We watch some new comedy on Netflix, both making jokes throughout. The whole bottle of wine is gone and so is our chinese food. After an intense laughing fit, Joshua cups my face in one of his hands. I lean into it, enjoying the feeling of someone else touching me.

"You are something else." I chuckle and feeling confident enough, I pull my opposite hand up to cradle his face, holding my wine glass in the other. His brown eyes dart between mine and my plump lips, a silent question. I lean in closer, whether it's the wine or my confidence tricking me, I press my lips to his. It starts slow, until he pushes against me forcefully tasting the sweet wine on my lips. It was going so good, feeling someone this close when it's been so long, until he adjusted against me and spilt the glass of wine over my shirt.

I gasp and pull back as he utters a curse. "Shit, Sam, I'm sorry." I shake my head and hold up a hand.

"It's fine, we've had a bit so it's sure to happen." He chuckles and takes my wine glass from me.

"The bathroom is down the hall to the right if you want to clean up a little, before we continue." He says the last quietly, with a ting of questioning in his voice. I nod and get up, making my way towards the bathroom.

Camille wasn't lying, I looked great and I felt just the same. The wine and atmosphere gave me a new sense of confidence, and maybe tonight could be the night I get laid. It's been a long time, and who says I can't have a little fun. I leave the bathroom and sneak out to the living room, but stop short at the corner when I hear Joshua on the phone, and rustling through my purse. "I'm trying to find it, she's dedicated to writing an article that will keep her there. If I could just find her notes and take some pictures of them, maybe I could get ahead." The confidence I was exuding strips from me in a millisecond. The candle lit dinner, wine and compliments were just a way to get information from me when I didn't expect it, getting laid could've just been a bonus.

"Fuck, it doesn't look like she brought it with her. But, I did find a box of condoms, who knew little Sam was so sultry. Maybe I'll get lucky at least one way tonight." My food feels like it's going to come up any second. I have to get out of here. I wipe the tears out of my eyes and fluff my hair before I turn a corner and shove him away from my belongings. The fear in his eyes is evident as I feel a flurry of anger spreading behind mine.

"You asshole!"

"Sam-" He tries to stand up but I shove him down to the ground.

"You self centered, idiotic prick! Stay away from me," I lean down closer, almost so our noses are touching and grab a fistful of his shirt, "And stay away from my fucking story." I let him fall back on the floor, grab my belongings and get the hell out of there.

I don't allow the tears to fall, instead I allow the anger to replace whatever embarrassment I felt moments ago. Wait till Camille and Francis hear about this, Joshua is going to have bigger problems than me.

SIXTEEN

Rowan

My flight did nothing to relieve my anger or Samara from my thoughts. I found myself across from her apartment, watching her and Camille pick out clothes. *Where is she going?* I turn my eyes away when I see Samara slip off her top, but not before I get a view of her black bra, contrasting with her beautiful skin. After a moment, I turn back to see her in a red blouse, form fitting jeans and heels. *Oh, hell no.* I unconsciously find myself walking to her apartment. I get in front of her door before she opens it, catching me by surprise and offering me no chance to rethink my decision. Her warm body slams into mine and I reach out to catch her as she does the same to steady herself. Her hazel eyes bore a hole into mine, and for a second I stop thinking about how she is probably dressing this nice to go meet someone.

I can't help my eyes as they glance up and down her body, the curves in her jeans being shown off to their not so full potential, but nobody else has to know that. "Where are you going?" It comes out faster and harsher than I wanted to, but I can tell it takes her aback. She removes herself from me and the warmth she provided is replaced by the lonely cold. "None of your business." She shoots it right back at me, causing me to tilt my head. This woman was dominant in her own way, she knows how to dish it out when she needs to. "Just asking." I retort, she glances at her watch and shakes her head. "I'm going to be late, whatever this is, it can wait." Sigh, she's definitely going on a date.

I follow her. Yes, I know, probably not a good idea considering my curiosity of her grows through every interaction. It doesn't take us long to end up at her destination, and I use my hearing to track her through the complex, finding a similar seat on a roof across from the apartment she's in. A short, average man greets her and I wonder what she sees in him. Throughout the night they eat, laugh, drink, talk and I think I might rip my hair out until he leans in to kiss her, and she kisses back. Then I think, that I might fly through his window and throw him out of it. He spills her glass of wine all over her blouse and she gets up to go to what I'm guessing is the bathroom to clean up. As soon as she is out of sight, my focus is on him and his focus is on whatever he's digging in her purse for. I listen in closer to the conversation he's having when he picks up his phone and dials someone.

"I'm looking for any notes or journals that she may have." That asshole. He was using her to get information, typical human. Greedy, selfish. *Like you?* The voice in my head pushes to the front and I shake it off, clearing those thoughts trying to continue listening. "I'm trying to find it, she's dedicated to writing an article that will keep her there. If I could just find her notes and take some pictures of them, maybe I could get ahead." I hear a separate heartbeat speed up, and I know Samara is just out of sight, catching him in the act. "Fuck, it doesn't look like she brought it with her. But, I did find a box of condoms, who knew little Sam was so sultry. Maybe I'll get lucky at least one way tonight." *Rage*, pure rage is all I feel as I narrow my eyesight on him. I could swoop down and throw him from his apartment before she could even see, but she turns a corner before I finish my thought. I don't have to listen in to tell she is giving him an earful, or watch closely to see that he is scared shitless. The last thing she does before she leaves is grab a handful of his shirt and pull him closer. His eyes grow so large I can practically see the whites of them from where I stand. She storms out of the apartment and hauls ass out of there. Calling a cab with a whistle and driving away.

That's my girl. Wait, what? I shake my head, absolutely not. My curiosity must stop, it's getting too far out of hand. The comfortability I feel with her, and the magnetic pull has to cease. This cannot happen again.

SEVENTEEN

Samara

Just as Camille said, she was back at her dad's when I got back to my apartment and I'm here by my lonesome. Walking to my bedroom, I strip the wine covered blouse off and begin to change. My anger slowly moved aside for the heartache to fit in. Sure, I knew Joshua was a self centered prick, he'd always been. But maybe, just maybe, he had a heart and truly wanted to move to a better, more linear slate.

My mind wanders to Camille, and I hope she never has to go through heartache with a boy, for his sake. I'd probably kill him if he just looked at her wrong, imagine breaking her heart.

Theo pops into my head, his disheveled black hair and those icy blue eyes. No doubt he's given his fair share of heartbreaks, he seems like the playboy type. I send Camille a text before I lay down to fall asleep.

I don't even bother showering, the night drained me more than I anticipated. The familiar sensation of being watched makes the hair stand up on my neck, but this time it isn't worrisome, it's comforting.

———————

My dream startles me awake and I feel like there's blood stuck to my skin. The screaming doesn't stop as the hair stands up on the back of my neck and I open my eyes wide, focusing on the city lights out the windows. Something feels wrong, really wrong. I turn over and grab my phone off the nightstand where it's charging. Missed calls, texts and alerts from Camille fill the screen. Some of them are pleas for help and others are just random letters typed together in a hurry. My heart falls to my stomach and then my throat begins to swell. I call her phone, once, twice and three times before I shoot up out of the bed and throw clothes on. I have to get to her.

Her location is still at her dad's. Her dad, Bradley, is a big guy. He stands at about six-foot-five and probably weighs more than three of me. Using the couple glances I've gotten of him, I decide in this instant that I cannot handle this alone. The adrenaline that is rushing through my body is nothing compared to his natural stature. As I slip on my shoes I look through the bathroom door and glance at Theo's jacket. Grabbing it as I dial his number on my phone. "What?" Great, he sounds mad already.

"Theo," I try to keep my voice from breaking, I don't want him thinking I'm weak. What am I kidding? This is Camille we are talking about.

"Look, I can't do this right now." I don't know who else to call, he has to help me with this. Not only is he intimidating all the time, but when he has to be, he's kind. I need that right now.

"Theo, please. I need you." I hate begging. I've only ever asked for help once, but to actually beg someone I barely know? I hear him take a deep breath and I have a little bit of hope for our situation.

"What's wrong?" I waste no time in replying, knowing that Camille could be hurt right now.

"It's Camille." The overwhelming feeling of guilt for allowing her to go and not checking up on her flows towards the surface.

"What do you mean?" His voice is slightly annoyed, but God only knows what kind of mood he was in before I called.

"She's in trouble. No time to explain. Meet me at the location I'm sending you." I hang up before he can reply and leave my apartment. The ride in the elevator is deafeningly silent as a million thoughts run through my head. The journey to Bradley's apartment is short, but feels like a lifetime. Different scenarios run through my head and allow me to think of the absolute worst possible endings to this night. Walking up to their building, I see Theo leaning up against a side rail looking bored. "You got here quickly."

"You called." The sincerity in his voice doesn't miss my ears, but the crashing sound of a bottle breaking fills whatever void I had left in my head.

I run up the stairs and through the hallways before I find Bradley's apartment, 23G. I hear drunken yelling and it sounds like someone is shuffling through trash. Theo is right behind me as I try to wiggle the door handle, it's locked. "Camille!" I yell as I put my forehead on the door, hoping she can feel me here.

"SAM!" Her voice makes me jerk the door back and forth trying to open it.

"Bradley, let me in you asshole!" Theo puts his hand on my shoulder, trying to stop me. I turn around and smack his hand off. "I didn't call you so you could tell me this was a bad idea. I called you so you can help me break down the door." He stares at me blankly before putting his hand back on my shoulder and tugging me to the side. In one swift motion, he throws his leg up and the door topples open inside the apartment.

Theo walks in first to scan the area, then moves so I can come in. My eyes land on Camille, cowering in a corner with her knees to her chest, hiding her face. My head whips over to a crash followed by a groan, to where I see Theo standing over Bradley. The apartment is covered in empty beer cans, cardboard boxes, and takeout containers. Frankly, the only thing I care about here is Camille. I turn back to her and try to cup her face with my hands. "Camille." She slowly lifts up to show me her face. I try not to flinch, but it's hard to try and hold my tears back. I bring my lips to her forehead as she begins to cry in my arms. Her face is beat black and blue and her eyes are puffy from crying. A broken lip pairs with the tears that are streaming down her face.

I walk her out of the apartment with Theo following behind me and he shuts the door, even though it's broken. The cab ride to my house is quiet, the sniffles of Camille keeps drawing us back to reality. Theo and I were sitting beside each other, while I leaned against Camille, trying to shield her from all the bad things that might come back to haunt her. I can't believe he would beat her. It's one thing to get angry at your child, but it's another to physically abuse them.

This moment has decided the future for Camille and I. I'm going to legally adopt her. Whatever hoops I have to jump through to ensure her safety and well-being, I will take care of them one by one, for her. Camille is softly sleeping by the time we get back to my apartment. I don't want to wake her up, so I nudge Theo with my arm and nod to Camille. He rolls his eyes and briefly smiles before he picks her up bridal style, with her head facing his body. We walk in silence until I open the doors for Theo to help put her down. We lay her in my bed and put the covers over her, being sure to be delicate. I feel like she's going to break at any moment.

Closing the door quietly, I turn to Theo who is now standing uncomfortably in the middle of my living room. "You look comfy." He turns to me and chuckles as I walk down the hallway towards him.

"It's a little different than I'm used to."

"How so? Preppy and preposterous?" I chuckle and he shakes his head.

"Light and welcoming." My heart flutters at his statement, and I realized, compared to some, my apartment does seem full of light and happiness. Completely opposite of Theo.

"Seems like it's not your style." He nods and continues to look around. "Do you want something to drink?" I turn and walk to the fridge, and hear him slightly shuffling behind me. I grab a water bottle and when I turn around he's right in front of me.

"Sure." The breath catches in my throat with him being so close. The warmth from his body surrounding me, pulling me in.

Before he turns and starts walking away from me, I grab his arm and say, "Thank you. For tonight."

He nods and replies, "No problem." I shake my head. He needs to know that saving Camille was important to me.

"I don't know what you said to Bradley, but-"

"I just told him if he ever sets his eyes on Camille again that I'd kill him. Or if he ever tried to find her here and got you involved I'd feed him to dogs."

My mouth hangs open and I try to decipher if he's being serious. "That was a lot."

"I'm a lot." He shrugs and acts like it isn't a big deal.

"Theo, I'm serious. This meant a lot to me, I'll make it up anyway that I have to so we are even."

"We don't have to be even, *Samara*. I did this for you. Accept it." There he goes, saying my name in that way and brushing it off like it's nothing. He looks at me with those deep blue eyes of his, and I feel like I can't breathe. The gentle sound of his breathing fills the silence in the room, and our eyes dart across each other's features. "I have to go." And with the blink of an eye, he's gone and away from me. And suddenly, the room fills with silence again while I feel empty.

EIGHTEEN

Rowan

The warmth of her breath is right in front of me, drawing me in closer. Her raven hair framing her hazel eyes that burrow into my soul, searching for something good in me. I didn't miss the shock when I told her what I explained to Bradley, I wonder if she thinks I was joking. I don't joke, especially about her. The touch of her hand on my arm, the sparks that travel through my body when she's near. I'm in deep trouble.

I take my leave quickly and make my way across the street to make sure she's okay being alone with Camille. Samara is pacing back and forth between the kitchen and the hallway connecting to her room, no doubt wanting to face Camille. When she gets confident enough to walk through the doors, Camille sits up and begins to sob. Samara runs to embrace her and

I can tell they will be alright for a night. I have to get her out of my head.

I decide to go to an old hangout of the fallen angels that was busted for drugs, prostitution, and pretty much anything else illegal that could happen in New York City. The Down Under was a rave spot that was run by some Australian werewolves; no doubt the pun was intended with the name. The entrance is an abandoned water facility. You can pick whichever sewer to go down, they all lead there. Rose and I used to come here all the time while we were hooking up. The drugs didn't really do anything but make us feel buzzed, our supernatural abilities makes it almost impossible for us to get drunk or high.

Even though this place was busted by an undercover agent a couple years ago, the fallen angels reclaimed it once Uriah, our mole in the police department, trashed evidence; effectively throwing out any case. The lights burn my eyes and the music feels like it's shaking my insides. This is one of the only places where the supernatural can be themselves: werewolves don't have to hide their claws, vampires can let their fangs grow, if I chose, I could let my wings out. I don't, though, not everyone needs to see them, plus they'd be inconvenient here. After a shapeshifter hands me something in a little baggie, I decided maybe to let loose tonight. *Samara was going to*. Fuck, I should not be thinking about that. I take whatever pills are in the bag and take a shot that's sitting beside me.

For a moment, nothing happens and it seems like time is frozen. Until I see raven hair move through the crowd, and for a second, I think it's her. I follow her through the crowd, pushing past all kinds of creatures, trying to get to her. *What's she doing here? What happened to Camille? How did she find this place?* All sorts of questions race through my head, but the one thought that doesn't leave is that she's in danger here. All kinds of creatures would love to have a taste of a human as beautiful as her.

The end of the crowd is in sight, and she turns down a hallway, leading me on a wild chase. "Samara!" My voice radiates authority and my mind doesn't think of the consequences of what happens if it is her. How will I explain what I'm doing here, what I am? I don't think twice about yelling her name a second time. "Stop!" She stops walking and by now we are on the backside of the bar, away from everyone. She turns, slowly, and faces me. I let out a breath I didn't know I was holding, the realization dawning on me that it's not her. This person has blood red eyes and her skin is pale, contrary to Samara's. The only thing similar is that raven head of hair they both sport. "Sorry, I thought you were someone else." I turn to leave but this girl grabs my elbow and turns me back around.

She flashes an award winning smile and says, "For you, baby, I can be whoever you want me to be." The shaking of the music stops and is replaced by a warm sensation that spreads throughout my body, a soft humming sound accompanies it.

Her body appears closer now and she starts to look more like Samara. Drawing me in, her hands come up to cup my face, despite the warm feeling, her hands are freezing. "I can be Samara, for you, *Rowan*." Her voice changes and I shiver at hearing Samara's voice say my name, my *real* name. She runs her arms up and down my side and then pulls me closer, so her hands are on my back. Lifting up my shirt, she reaches up to the scars on my back from my wings, and I reach down to kiss her. Her lips, covered in that red lipstick, are soft, but they don't fit me well. Instead, they feel slimy and salty.

I pull back and instead of meeting Samara's hazel eyes, the red ones are staring back at me. Her face is now in her natural state, decaying, decomposing. "Theo," She whispers, bringing me back to the reality where Samara doesn't know my real name. I push her off of me as hard as I can and she hits the wall that sits behind us.

I wrap my hand around her throat, "Siren."

She scoffs and tries to take a breath in, "Estella is the name." I push in her throat just a little more before I release her and step back. "Come on, Rowan. Everyone knows you're down for a good time. If she's who you want to see, we can make that happen."

"Leave me be." I turn to walk away and she's already in front of me.

"I can see everything in that sexy, little mind of yours." Chilling, knowing someone can see into the deepest parts of my mind without my consent. "I know who you're looking for. I also know where you can find him."

NINETEEN

Samara

With the absence of Theo, the elephant in the room begins to scream at me. It's my fault for this. I told Camille she should go see her dad. If I had been a better guardian, or just been awake when she called me, I could've been there so much faster. I pace back and forth between my kitchen and the entrance to my room, what if she feels the same way I do? What if she doesn't want to stay here anymore? Where would she go?

No. I did the best I could. I think to myself as I gain confidence and walk straight to the bedroom. When the door opens, Camille is awake. She sits up and whines while adjusting herself. Once we lock eyes, she starts to sob and I run to cradle her. "I am never leaving you again." I tell her softly as I hold her head against my chest. She cries to her heart's content, muttering silent apologizes. After quite some time, her breathing becomes normal again, and she sits up to wipe her face. "You don't have to talk about it." I assure her, if it's too much, I would rather her take her time.

"No, I've needed to tell you too." Oh shit, this does nothing for my anxiety.

"Take your time." I sit cross legged in front of her on the bed, she's still wrapped up in the blankets and her face is puffy from her crying. I grab a box of tissues from the nightstand and wait for her to start talking.

"He was doing so well. As far as I know, he'd been sober for almost a month." That was good for a man who was a functioning alcoholic; someone who always had a beer in his hand. "We went out for breakfast at that Cafe down in Brooklyn." I know the one she's talking about. It's the one where her mom and dad met, it holds significant value to them. "I like someone from school. I decided to tell him, but his demeanor changed immediately." What's so bad about having a crush? "He got up and left me there. I took the train home." That asshole. I always knew he wasn't a good person, but for the sake of Camille, I was glad he was trying.

"When I got home, he had already been through a twelve pack. I tried to reason with him." The sobbing comes back. "I tried apologizing, and taking it back. He wouldn't listen. He slapped me first." I take a deep breath, trying to keep it together and not turn around to go kill him. "I fell down afterwards, and he pulled me up by my hair. He started muttering my mom's name." The thought was always in the back of my head that Bradley would do the same thing to his wife. I do my best not to show this thought on my face, Camille doesn't need another reminder.

"All of this for liking someone, Camille. Why would he act this way?" She makes eye contact with me and then looks away. Clearing her throat, she mutters it so quietly I almost miss it.

"Because it's a girl."

I smile softly, and reach my hand up to cup her face. "And you know that's okay, right?" She breaks down into sobs again and throws her arm around me to hug me.

"You aren't mad at me?"

I shake my head and rub her back softly, "Camille, I'm proud of you for telling me." I pull her in closer and continue, "You are the best thing in my life, I consider you my own. You telling me this means that you trust me more than him. If you didn't trust me, you wouldn't tell me why the fight started, or even what happened." We adjust on the bed so she is laying on my chest and I am leaning against the headboard. "I will protect you until my last dying breath, hell, I would probably be dead without you."

She chuckles softly, "I guess we're even now."

Her joke about that night makes me chuckle. "Yeah kiddo, we're even." There was someone else I needed to get even with too: Theo. I turn on the television and put some random movie on, shortly after,

Camille is fast asleep. No doubt she's worn out from everything we've been through today. I slip out from under her and pull the covers up past her shoulders.

Shutting the bedroom door quietly, I find my phone and scroll through my contacts until Theo's name pops up. Dialing it, I sit on the couch and put my back against the armrest. I almost think he won't answer, he was just here what feels like mere moments ago. "Samara?" His voice finally comes through and I let out a sound of relief, he must have saved my number, too. I hear the bass of club music behind him, I turn to look at the time: 1:45a.m.

"Are you at a club right now?"

He lets out a sigh, "What? Don't expect it from me?"

"A pain in the ass, violent private investigator? Seems right up your alley." I hear him chuckle and the music starts to die out, I'm assuming he is walking out from wherever he is.

"How is Camille?" I smile softly and glance back to the closed bedroom door.

"Well, we've cried a lot, laughed a bit, and now she's asleep."

"I want to beat him up again."

Even though he can't see me, I smile and nod my head. "Yeah, especially for this reason: Camille has a crush on a girl." I hear Theo scoff, knowing good and well we're probably on the same page. It seems like we would be on the same wavelength.

"Hey," he says softly, "How are you?" My smile falters for only a second. Worry consumes me as my head goes between the serial killer, keeping my job, protecting, and adopting Camille.

"As good as can be expected. I actually called to thank you again, and to see what I could do to make it up to you?"

My voice goes higher as I realize how he might take it, a playboy like himself. "I already told you, we don't have to get even. I did it for you."

"Yeah but like, what if I buy you dinner or something?" I chuckle but he's quiet on the other line: apparently he didn't share the same light heart. "Forget it, I was just-"

"Sure."

My mouth hangs open slightly and I let out a breath. "What?"

"Let's get dinner." He says it confidently, and I can't tell if he's got a smile on his face or not.

"Alright-"

"How about tomorrow?" I smile and don't say anything for a moment. "Samara?"

"You know you can call me Sam, right? Everyone else-"

He clears his throat and cuts me off, "I like your name. I also like being the only one who calls you that."

I chuckle slightly, "My Mom also calls me that."

"Dinner, tomorrow night. I'll pick you up."

TWENTY

Rowan

My hands are sweaty and I feel like there's a lump in my throat. What the hell was I thinking? The words were just flowing out of my mouth when I agreed to dinner. The conversation with the siren, Estella, was fresh in my head even though it was yesterday.

"What are you talking about?" My face contorts in anger, and I shove her away from me. She keeps closing the distance, but I know if she gets too close she'll be able to get into my head again.

"I was in your head for a solid forty-five seconds. That gave me plenty of time to see all your vile little thoughts." My mind goes back to taking Mekaia's spot, the late nights spent with Rose, and my consuming curiosity with Samara. "I know all about you and that humans' search for whatever is killing those people."

"And what? You think you know something I don't?" She scoffs and shakes her head, finally taking a step back from me to lean against a pillar.

"I always know something others don't." In the form she chose, she's no doubt attractive. She's short and thin, but her face is delicate and her blood red eyes stick out sorely from the complexion of her skin. Her raven hair reminds me of Samara, no doubt helping to lead me into a trap.

"Don't play coy, you're just doing this because I know what you are and broke from your spell."

"Something only a handful of souls can do." She's definitely stronger than I am, she's probably double my age. *"Throughout my life, I've had plenty of poor soldiers who have served me. Unfortunately, for me, you won't be one of them."* She pushes off the pillar and comes closer, dragging her long nail across my pecs as she circles me. *"You're already a slave to another."* When I turn to grab her hand, she disappears and laughs from in front of me once more.

"I am no one's slave."

"No? Then why do you take Mekaia's failing sickness? Why do you repeatedly serve him when you know you are a better fit? Why is your mind swirling around some petty human g-" I reach forward with my speed and finally pin her, putting my knee between her legs and holding her throat, similar to the predicament we were in just a moment ago.

"Don't you dare say her name, or I will rip your heart out and end this pathetic existence of what you call a life."

I can tell that she is now frightened. Her arms thrash at mine to get it off her throat. "I can help!" She manages to wheeze out the one sentence I can't ignore. I let go of her and move backwards, keeping my distance.

"Start talking." She falls to the ground and begins to cough, I guess I put a little more pressure than I thought.

"I already know about your meeting with Jeckel, but there's one person you haven't met with that's crucial to your investigation." I tilt my head slightly, and urge her to keep talking with my hand. "The black market is secret, but to a supernatural club downtown, it's a direct path there. Whether you become a customer, or their object, you make your way in." New York City, the best place to go missing, has a simple club to pick off humans to traffic them. Not surprising. "The boss, Killian, handpicks both customers and objects. Some say that he has a boss who influences his decisions. The person who truly picks people out." I know what she's thinking, and it's hard to think about the best way to handle it. "You get close to someone who attracts Killian's eyes, you find the big boss."

Now, standing in front of Samara's door, I know good and well that we won't be able to keep the topic of the investigation off the table. Then, knowing myself, I won't be able to stop and tell her what I've found out. I knock three times on her door rather hard, and it swings open, revealing Samara, who looks like she just jumped out of a cookbook. Her hair is pulled back but some pieces fall to frame her face. She's wearing a light color pair of jeans with a tan top and her cardigan she wears when I watch her. *She likes that thing,* I think to myself. I chuckle, and pull the bottle of wine from behind my back. Her face morphs into a full teeth smile as she grabs it and my hand, pulling me inside. Her apartment smells of gravy and green beans. I look towards the kitchen and she reads my mind. "I'm making dinner. Decided to show you a taste of my hometown's cooking."

"Oh yeah? Where exactly are you from?"

She smiles and stirs something on the stove. "Some small town in Kentucky."

"Kentucky? Wouldn't have picked little miss reporter for a country girl."

She shakes her head and points to a cabinet, "Wine stuff is in there." I walk over and grab an opener and two glasses, filling them halfway. "Little miss reporter wanted to get out of her hometown after her dad died." The conversation turns sour. Living for as long as I have, death is pretty natural for me, but I forget how permanent it is for humans. One moment and the rest of their life is taken away, their loved ones grieve and essentially, the world can stop for some.

"I'm sorry to hear that."

She nods and is quiet for a minute. "Pretty shitty way to start off dinner." She reaches up high to grab some plates, barely reaching them. I decided to walk over and close her in with my body behind hers.

Setting her wine glass down beside her, I reach over her head and grab two of the plates she was reaching for.

"Why keep them up so high if it's just you and Camille?" She shivers, my mouth is by the top of her head and I know she must feel the warmth of my breath.

"We usually have takeout."

"So you're testing your cooking abilities on me?"

She chuckles and moves to take the plates from me, "I couldn't get this recipe out of my head even if I tried." She begins to plate and I make my way over to the counter, setting our glasses down accordingly: me facing the door and her facing the city. I watch her plate meticulously, once finished she walks over and sets them down in front of me. Walking back around to grab her wine glass, she begins to speak, "Chef Allen, reporting for duty." I chuckle and watch her as she comes to sit beside me. "Here we have an after church special: hamburger steak and gravy along with mash potatoes and green beans. Unfortunately, I don't have any bread, so you're missing out just a little."

The food smells delicious and with a little more staring from her, I put a forkful into my mouth. The southern charm evident in her cooking, I close my eyes and savor the taste. I can't remember the last time I had a home cooked meal. "Well?" I turn to meet those eyes I can't resist as she looks at me and shakes her head. "You can't eat my cooking and then not tell me what you think."

I take a sip of my wine and laugh, "It's one of the best meals I've ever had."

"Well, now you're just saying that because I asked." We laugh loudly together and begin to enjoy our meal. We talk sparingly, enjoying each other's company, but I learn a bit about her. She graduated top of her class and got a scholarship to college. Her father died when she was eighteen. After graduation, a drunk driver crashed into him and ran. They never found him. She used that time to bring attention to drunk driving, and even won a journalism contest, which put her on the radar of Shapiro Informatics. Basically, it's how she got her ticket to New York City.

Of course, I had to be limited with the details of my life. I tried not to lie, but it was hard when I was already pretending to be Theo. I wish I could tell her the truth, not only would it keep her safe and not in the dark, but maybe give her more ideas about the case we're working on. "What's wrong?" I realize I've gone quiet and now she is staring at me, wondering what I'm thinking.

I turn the conversation to something we are both familiar with, "I got a lead on the case. I don't want to spoil our-" She pushes her plate away, grabs her wine glass and walks over to the couch.

"Sit and spill." This woman.

I follow her over with less enthusiasm. "One of my contacts in the party scene told me about a club that's downtown called NightHawk. She said it's basically the entrance way into the black market."

"Meaning that's where buyers go?" I nod and get more comfortable, bringing one of my knees under me, it brushes against hers and it doesn't go unnoticed when the warmth spreads from the contact. She takes a breath in and for a second I think she's going to move her leg. She doesn't.

"Buyers and the product. The manager of the club, Killian, is the one who picks them. But my contact says even he has a boss who influences his decisions."

"We find Killian, we find the boss working the black market."

I nod, "In theory, we find the boss who knows our murderer."

She jumps up, shocking me for a minute and puts her wine glass down, no doubt feeling a little tipsy. "Let's go. Right now."

TWENTY ONE

Samara

"Fuck no." Theo's brazenness takes me aback.

"What do you mean no? This is a lead, Theo! This is what we've been waiting for!"

He stands with me, towering over my smaller frame, "Absolutely not. End of discussion."

"Why?" I protest, putting my hands on my hips. The movement is noticeable to him as he looks me up and down before he lets out a breath and runs his hands through his hair.

"When they see you, of all people, they're going to want to pluck you right up. I don't know this place, how am I supposed to protect you?" I breathe deeply. He's so worried about protecting me, what about the innocent people who have died.

"Not only will we be able to get a first look at the leaders of this black market, we might get a shot at getting evidence to report them and stop this. People have died, Theo!"

He nods slowly and looks from me, to the city through the windows in my apartment. "I will only do this if you let me have some sort of backup there."

"What kind of backup does a private investigator have?"

He smirks at me, "You don't know everything about me, Samara." He steps closer, emphasizing my name. "First things first, and I mean no offense by this," I'm gonna take offense. "You are not going to draw attention in a club looking like that."

My mouth falls agape and I look down at my outfit. I close my mouth, he's right. Although, I have the perfect outfit for this. "Fine, I'll be right back." I leave him in the living room and make my way to my room. Rummaging through my closet to the back, I find the dress I had in mind, a perfect outfit for this club: skimpy and sultry. A short, black dress with see through long sleeves and a three ring cut out between my breasts. I put on a pair of black lace up heels and let my hair down, I've never had to do much with it when it's natural. I put on a bit of red lipstick, and suddenly I'm self conscious. I've just now connected the dots that Theo is right outside my door. What is he going to think of me? This dress still had the tags on it until just now, I never wear clothes like this. Camille had given this to me as a birthday gift a year ago.

I shake off those thoughts and open my bedroom door, Theo has his back turned to me and is on the phone with someone. "We are leaving now, be there soon." He turns around as he hangs up and goes still. His eyes rake up and down my body shamelessly before looking me in the eyes. His blue eyes have gone dark, and I wonder if I've made a mistake. "You look-"

"It's too much isn't it? I just figured with us going to a club and wanting to attract attention that I should-"

He holds up his hand and smiles softly, "You look beautiful."

My heart flutters. "Let's go." He says with authority and I write a note for Camille. She said she was hanging out with some friends, so I fix her plate and put it in the microwave. 'Food in the microwave, don't wait up!' I put a heart along with my initials and head out the door. Following Theo's large frame, we get into the elevator and the ride down is silent. We are silent the whole way to the club in the cab and I begin to see homeless people sitting on the road by the time we get to our destination.

It surprises me that some people come to clubs like this. NightHawk is written in neon letters above an entryway to a brick building, and there's no line at the door. Knowing the history of this place now, they probably want to stuff as many people in here as possible. A long list of victims and enough drunk people to not notice. Theo hands the guy a twenty dollar bill, and we both receive stamps on our hand. Theo gets a glowing white hawk, and when I reach up my hand for the same one the bouncer shakes his head. "No, you get this one." He reaches in his pocket and picks up a different stamp. My stamp is a pair of angel wings that glow pink. I look up at Theo and he grabs my hand to lead me inside.

The strobe lights already affect my vision and the music makes me feel like I'm floating. "I think they've already made you a target." Theo leans down and presses his mouth close to my ear so I can hear. I close my eyes as his breath hits my body, fanning me with its warmth. His body is close and smells of peppermint, with a lingering waft of our dinner.

"Why?" He grabs my hand to hold it to my face, and then nods his head to a group in what seems to be the VIP lounge. A group of men in tuxedos are looking in our direction. I look back up to Theo, he lets go of me and takes a step away.

"Trust me." He mouths. I nod my head and make my break to the bar.

The bodies of people pressing against me make me fly out my comfort zone. I have to do this, I think to myself. Once I reach the bar, a man, the bartender, walks up in front of me. "What can I get the pretty lady?"

I smile softly and flip my hair so it's behind my back, showing off my neck. "How about your name?" I try to turn the charm up and I think I'm failing, until he shows a full smile of teeth and chuckles. He's attractive no doubt, he's mixed with a nose ring and a buzzcut. His teeth are pearly white as he chuckles and leans in on his elbows.

"My name's Uriah, what's yours?" My smile falters and I remember the conversation Theo and I had with Jeckel. Uriah was the detective that told Jeckel to keep quiet about the murders. He notices this and glances behind me briefly before returning to my gaze. "Everything okay?"

I nod and smile once more. "My name is Sam."

"Well, *Sam*, what can I get you?" My name sounds like venom on his tongue and I don't like it, it's nothing compared to how Theo says it. He opens his arms and gestures to the full bar. Even though I've already had some wine this evening, with this atmosphere, I've already sobered up.

"Just a club soda for me, please."

He shakes his head, "Oh come on, you're here of all places and you want a nonalcoholic drink?"

I sigh and roll my shoulders back. "Fine, a shot of tequila for me, chilled."

"Salt and lime?"

I nod and glance around while replying, "You know it." I've lost sight of Theo, but know better than to think he isn't keeping an eye on me. He's probably making his own rounds, asking about Killian and looking at the exits around the club.

"One tequila shot, chilled for the lady, Sam." I turn back around to meet Uriah's eyes once again.

"How much?"

"On the house, per our manager, Killian." Hearing Killian's name sends chills down my spine. I've been here less than five minutes and I'm already managing to catch their attention. I wonder how many other girls have faced the same. Uriah taps the headphone in his ear and points behind me. I follow his finger to the VIP lounge Theo and I saw when I walked in. "You should thank him in person, he's not always this generous."

Fantastic, I was making a psycho generous. I down the shot and chase it with the lime immediately, I need this liquid courage for what I'm about to do next. Without another glance towards Uriah, I turn and strut to the VIP lounge. One man sticks out. He looks to be a little older with his silver hair, and for some reason he's wearing sunglasses while in here. "Are you Killian?"

Two bodyguards block my path to him and he waves them off, "Yes, my dear. Did you enjoy my present?" Does this man think a way to lure someone in is to pay for a seven dollar shot?

"Yes, very thoughtful. Although, your bartender tells me you aren't always generous. Why me?" I step down into the lounge and make my way past the other men that are there, trying not to notice their gazes up and down my bare legs. Killian pats the empty spot beside him. As I sit down, his hand grips my waist and I resist the urge to vomit.

"Have you seen the way you look tonight?" I know I look good, but hearing him compliment me makes me want to put on my pajamas and burn this dress. "You know, I have a penthouse above the club. I think you'd enjoy it." Knowing good and well that it's probably a bad decision, but more so an important part of the investigation, I make a split second decision to agree.

"I'd love to see it." Killian rises from his seat and grabs my hand roughly, leading me to an elevator. We get inside and before the doors close, I catch a glimpse of Theo trying to push through the crowd. My heart drops knowing that from now on, until Theo finds a way up to this penthouse, I am alone.

TWENTY TWO

Rowan

As Samara walks through the club and to the VIP lounge that has Killian and his other accomplices, I take this moment to go debrief with Uriah. "That girl got spunk."

"Did she say anything?" He shakes his head no, but stops wiping down a glass and turns to me.

"She knew my name, I saw it in her eyes. Did you tell her anything?" First Rose, now Uriah, thinking that I can't keep our secret or that I would commit treason against our kind.

"She probably remembers your name from our first interrogation with another witness. You might remember him, name's Jeckel."

He sighs and glances over to her, "You're deep in this shit, you know."

I nod, "Mekaia told me to figure it out. That's exactly what I'm doing." He fixes me a cup of water and I chug it. Only having alcohol before this was not a good idea, I have to be alert, especially with Samara involved. "Thanks for coming and being back up."

"Hey, you need someone. Not saying knocking out the bartender and serving shitty drinks is my speciality, but you picked the right person for this job." We chuckle for a moment before we both look back over to see Samara and Killian gone from the lounge.

"Where is she?" I look around frantically. I can't let anything happen to her, for Camille's sake, that is.

"There!" Uriah's voice draws me out and I see them entering the elevator. I push through people and try to get there before it closes. I could take care of the two bodyguards and get her out of here before she's in any real danger. When our eyes meet, I hope she doesn't see the panic in mine when I realize that the doors are closing before I can get there, and that she is on her own until I figure out a way up there.

"Rowan!" I turn to meet Uriah coming from behind the bar, his face morphs to confusion as he looks at me. He sees the panic in my eyes, and he knows what it means even if I don't.

"Tell me how to get up there." He lets out a huff and motions for me to follow him outside. Both of us weave through the drunken crowd and the fresh air hits us in the face, I feel like I can breathe again. It's not as smooth as when I know she's safe, but she will be soon.

"Straight up, that's your way in." Uriah points one of his fingers up and I see lights coming from a penthouse at the top.

"I don't even want to think about what's on all those floors." The bar itself looks pretty rundown on the outside, but has been completely renovated on the inside. I'm not sure how many floors this place has, but I can be sure illegal and disgusting activities happen on each one.

Uriah's wings stretch out from behind his shirt and he rolls his shoulders back. He's fairly new to life as a fallen angel, he's only been down for a century now. Letting your wings out becomes easier, less painful, through time. "Wait," I grab his arm and stop him before he takes off. "Samara doesn't know what we are. You guys have been bickering with me about keeping our secret, yet you just want to fly up there and save her?" Rich, they can do it but I can't? Hypocrites. As much as I would like to get her out of there with my powers, I know that it would just make this experience more confusing for her, and put my kind at risk. Uriah retracts his wings and shrugs his shoulders.

"Well, what do you expect we will do?" His voice is a challenge, to see how I hold up as a leader under pressure. Not only can I not let Samara down, I can't have Uriah thinking I'm weak.

"The fire escapes, it won't take us long to get up there. Plus it gives us an advantage to see what we're up against." He nods and we begin up the fire escape. With our speed and strength, it doesn't take long to reach the penthouse level. I raise my head slightly over the ledge and take a look at the outdoor area that has a pool. Several people are here, in fact, most of them look to be human. This is probably where Killian takes the victims so his boss can look at them and pick through them like cattle.

"She's over there." I follow Uriah's gaze and see an uncomfortable looking Samara surrounded by Killian and what looks to be more of his goons. Killian has his hands on her waist and is making her sit on his lap, his hands wander and I see Samara trying to push them down. *Rage*, similar to the rage I felt watching her with her date a couple nights ago. Except this time, these guys are definitely going to die. Glancing around, I don't see many bodyguards. Just the two Killian came up with in the elevator, except they're spread out and focusing more on the humans in the pool. "We can easily jump up, grab Killian and the girl and get the hell out of here."

I look at him quizzically, "What are you talking about? We have to help these people."

"It's going to be Killian and the girl, or everyone else. We can't do both." Deep down, I know he's right. There's only two of us and too many humans to count.

On top of it, we don't even know what kind of creature Killian is. We have to be careful about this.

I know I'm stronger than Uriah; it comes with my size and my age. I know I have to be the one to grab Killian, but everything in me wants to forget about the investigation, grab her, and fly as fast as my wings can carry me. Unfortunately, I know that's not how this is going to go. "Alright, you grab Samara. Protect her over anything." Uriah furrows his brows at me, it goes against everything in us to truly protect someone other than ourself and our own kind, but with him listening intently, I know he understands. "Anything goes sideways, anyone slips, you get out of there. I'll take care of Samara, that's my main concern."

"What does she mean to you?"

The question rings in my ears and I shake my head, trying my best to play it off. "Can't have a reporter showing up dead when investigating the same murders. She's my way to figure this out." I feel his gaze shift away from me and I focus my attention back onto her.

"Rose isn't going to like that." I chuckle and move my body to a crouch, this way it will be easier to jump to them.

Using all the strength I have, I jump and use my speed to end up right in front of Killian, throwing Samara off his lap and into Uriah's arms. She stands there, mouth agape, looking between both of us. I can blame this on her drinking, saying her shot was spiked. Better than watching eight foot wings sprout out of my back. I grab Killian by his throat and hoist him up to my eye level. He's a shorter man, so his legs dangle below him as he struggles to breathe. "I'll only ask once, who do you work for?"

With what air he has left, he chuckles and says, "You'll never live to see it."

The earth feels as if it's shaking and I drop Killian. In the blink of an eye, where he once was is now a black mass, swirling in the wind. "Rowan! He's possessed!" I hear Samara shuffle against Uriah, he lets her go. What the hell is he thinking? He spreads his wings and flies out of here. I am tempted to follow, but I have gotten no information and Samara is still here with me. Her screams are now louder and I realize that the bodyguards have come and grabbed her, one on each side. I turn to charge towards them but am held back by this demon. It's holding my arms behind my back, and when I glance over my shoulder to look at it, I'm met with Killian once again. Except this time, his eyes are bleeding from his sockets. So Killian was a human? Probably someone's grandparent who was in the wrong place at the wrong time. Now, he's possessed by a demon.

"A little birdy told me you care for this girl." He uses his hand, which has now decayed, to move my face towards Samara.

I begin to thrash against him with all my might, to no avail, when I see the body guards dragging Samara against the edge of the railing. Uriah is gone and she is my responsibility, I have to get to her. "Wonder how you'd feel if she was flat on her back?" With that, the bodyguards lift her effortlessly and toss her over the side of the building. My heart plummets to the ground and something between a cry and a roar comes out of me. My wings rip through my clothing and launch me away from Killian, off the roof and towards her, as fast as I can go. When I see her, she's halfway to the ground, I push my wings, one, two, a third time and we're almost face to face. Tears stain her cheeks and her hair is flowing wildly around her. If this was a different time, I'd probably compliment her beauty. All I can think about now, though, is the thought of watching her body hit the ground and the life fading out of her hazel eyes. *You can't die, you won't.*

We're moving in slow motion now, I reach out an arm to grab her, she reaches out her hand; and I miss.

TWENTY THREE

Samara

The whole elevator ride consisted of Killian either feeling me up, complimenting me, or telling me all about his expensive penthouse. God, Theo, I hope you have a plan because I'm all out of magic tricks.

When the elevator doors open, I'm surprised at the difference between the club and the penthouse. Elegance at home is what this feels like. If I didn't know the people involved here, I'd say it looks like any preppy rich kid movie. Killian leads me out onto the patio where there's a party going on. Drunk people are dancing and swimming in the pool; this looks like it's leading to a disaster.

"My dear," He sits down and puts his hands on my waist, pulling my body into his. "You are in for a treat." Oh no. His voice sends shivers down my spine and it turns into a raspy chainsmoker voice. When I turn back over to meet his eyes, I get a glimpse of red. Something is definitely wrong with him, is he sick? Of course he's sick in the head, but maybe it's a disease. Please for the love of God, do not tell me I am in the start of the zombie apocalypse. "You can stay with me here for the rest of your life, you'll feel like you're on cloud nine all the time." He's probably referring to drugs he gives his victims to make them docile. I wiggle in his grasp but he just pulls me closer, the feeling of him flushed against my body is enough to make me want to gag. The smell of sulfur fills my nostrils and it makes me dizzy.

I blink and I feel a sudden warmth until it's gone. When my eyes open, I see Theo standing between Killian and I. The bartender, Uriah, has a hold of me. Theo turns and looks at me, silently looking me over to make sure I'm in one piece. How did he get here so fast? Where did he even come from? The elevator never opened and there's no way they could've scaled the side of the building that fast. I struggle against Uriah's grasp, with no success.

Theo grabs Killian by his throat and I gasp; I've seen Theo get physical with someone before, but it looks as if he could really hurt this guy. I always thought his facade was just something he put up to seem more intimidating. Alas, maybe it's for real. Killians legs start to flail around as he's lifted up higher than he can stand, I almost feel sorry for him. Almost. "I'll only ask once, who do you work for?" Theo's voice sounds dark, and even looking at his backside, I can tell his eyes are menacing. I hear Killian chuckle and my stomach drops, something's wrong.

"You'll never live to see it."

It feels as if an earthquake begins, the water in the pool starts to shake and the partiers have finally realized what's going on. Where Killian was standing, a black cloud emerged and the smell of sulfur intensified for me. "Rowan! He's possessed!" Uriah shouts in Theo's direction. Rowan? What the fuck is going on? Who are these people, really? I struggle against Uriah once more, and this time, he lets me go. I think about making a break for the stairs or the elevator until large wings sprout from Uriah's back and he flies off the building. The lump in my throat grows and I think a scream leaves my mouth but I'm not sure; all I hear is arguing and ringing.

I feel strong hands grab my arms and come back to reality. The reality where the two bodyguards now have me held hostage and are walking to the side of the building. Theo, Rowan, whoever this man is, begins to thrash against Killian. I don't understand why he's trying to get away until I see Killian whisper something in his ear, and I feel the floor slip from under me. It doesn't take me long to feel the wind around me and realize I am falling. From however tall this building is, life is moving in slow motion for me. I hear a scream, and I truly believe it to be my own. *You can't die, you won't.* My consciousness sounds different but I'm too preoccupied by my thoughts as I fall through the air. Will Camille find the will under my bed? What's going to happen with these murders? Will my mother die of grief when they say I killed myself? Am I about to meet my father once again? What will Francis and Joshua do? Does Theo, or Rowan, feel guilty for not protecting me?

I see him, flying through the air towards me, the same wings are behind him as they were on Uriah. I stare at him, and finally allow myself to admire his regal beauty, as I think it will be the last face I see before I die. He's getting closer, his wings flap in the wind and he is close enough to reach an arm out to me. I guess I've been falling long enough that when I reach out and miss his arm, that I should meet my end any second.

No. The voice in my head returns and I throw out my other arm and turn my body. I feel his hand connect with mine and it feels like he uses all his strength to bury me into his chest. The warmth engulfs me, and I realize now we are going upwards instead of falling down. He cradles my body bridal style and I dig my head into his chest. I don't care about anything else right now except that I am alive. At least, I think I am.

This thought quickly fades when I gain confidence to look at where we are. The wind blowing in my hair should've been a clear indication that we are still somehow in the air. When I see his wings flap once more, I scream. He tightens his grip on me and lets me scream. I've officially gone crazy. The blood that rushed to my brain along with my adrenaline during my fall has caused me to hallucinate.

After screaming so much I end up passing out, or at least I hope I did, because when I open my eyes, I'm in what looks to be a dark studio apartment. It looks almost exactly like mine, but instead of light and welcome, it's dark and mysterious.

I'm laying in someone's bed, with a long shirt draped over my dress. I say someone, because Theo, Rowan, whoever he is, is sitting at the foot of the bed, watching me. I sit up fast and my head spins. "Be easy, you've been through a lot tonight."

"Who the hell are you?" I close my eyes and talk. Mostly because I know if I look him directly in the eyes that I may forgive any and everything that happened tonight, but also because my brain feels like it's banging against my skull. He sighs and when I open my eyes he is staring directly into them. He looks sad, the kind of sad kids get when you tell them they can't have the toy they see at the store.

"Samara," He says my name and it makes me realize that I am alive and that this is real. "We need to have a serious conversation."

"There's nothing to talk about. You lied to me and I want nothing to do with you." He flinches at the harshness displayed in my voice. I've had my fair share of betrayals the last couple nights, and this one almost caused my death. "You knew what we were walking into. You were secretive and didn't want to let me in and it almost got me killed tonight."

He scoots closer just as I scoot farther back into the headboard. He lets out a breath and stands up, walking over to a table and grabbing a chair. He picks it up, walks back over to the bed and puts the chair right beside me. Sitting down, he speaks to me softly, "I'll tell you anything you want to know."

TWENTY FOUR

Rowan

"What's your name?" I chuckle at her first question. Out of everything she went through tonight, seeing a demon, finding out I lied to her, almost dying, and getting an up close look at my wings, she wants to know the most innocent question. This woman is something else.

"Rowan."

She stares at me blankly and shakes her head, "That's it? No last name?"

I shake my head, "We don't get last names."

"We?" I nod, quickly realizing this conversation was going to take a while, but I was going to let her set the speed. Rushing her into all this may just make her spiral.

"What was with that sulfur smell? And that black smoke coming from Killian? And the wings that you and the bartender have? Am I going crazy?"

Jumping right in, I see. I take a deep breath and she looks at me intuitively. "To answer your questions, I'm going to have to give you a bit of a background." She nods and sits up a bit more, unconsciously moving closer to me. It takes everything in me not to pull her onto my lap and hold her there. Catching her with barely a second to lose, makes me think of all the possibilities in which tonight could have ended. I leave her be and explain it the best I know how.

"All those scary stories you grew up listening to about supernatural creatures, all of them are true. Vampires, werewolves, sirens, witches. Everyone that you can think of from some fairy tale, are all reality." I stop briefly and let her soak that in, but she just looks at me, so I continue. "Tonight, Killian was a regular human who was possessed by a demon. You probably smelled sulfur tonight around him, that's a key component in realizing a demon is nearby."

"Was he always like that?"

She interrupts me but with a genuine question, I smile softly, "No. Killian was once a regular human. When the demon decides he is finished with him, he will be nothing but an empty shell."

"Why Killian? What does a demon look for when finding someone?" I shake my head, her questions are good, but they make me feel even more guilty than I already do. I shouldn't be telling her any of this.

"Most demons look for someone in a state of power, wealth, or beauty. Some humans who figure out the lore want to be possessed. They say it gives a euphoric feeling all the time."

She sits up straighter and gasps, "He mentioned something about being on cloud nine and staying there forever. Is that what he meant?"

The idea of another supernatural creature being close enough to cause that makes my hair stick up and my skin boil. I nod slowly and explain. "Killian's body is probably getting worn out by the second. That demon felt powerful and probably needed a new host. Why not the sexiest girl in the club?" I don't miss the blush she has when she has to look away. I don't know what this feeling is or why I keep saying these things, but knowing I can make her look like that makes me feel something I've never felt before.

"Well, what are you? And what do you have to do with the murders?"

The question I've been waiting for. No human in my lifetime or the next should know anything about this, and she's about to be the first. "I am a fallen angel."

She chuckles a little, "Is this supposed to be a pick-up line?"

My face remains serious, and despite how proud she is of herself, she clears her throat and motions towards me to continue. "Fallen Angels are the top of the food chain in the supernatural world. Everyone else is made from the Devil, but we are made from God himself."

"So Heaven and Hell actually exist?" I nod. She should not know this, nothing good ever comes of it.

"Fallen angels are heavenly angels that have been cast out. My wings are black on Earth, but in Heaven, they're white."

"What's the reason for getting cast out?"

I shake my head and look down at my hands. They're clasped together and look white as snow. "Broke the rules. Did something we weren't supposed to. One slip up and you're gone."

She looks saddened by this. "I've messed up plenty, and I've never gotten kicked out of anywhere."

I smile softly at her. "Heaven has a hard line."

"That's surprising." Her response makes me chuckle. Such a feisty human for just learning about the scary stories. "What was it like up there?"

I shake my head, "I don't know. They wipe your memory when you're cast down. You can't even remember the reason you were cast out. You have to find out on your own."

"How?" *Pressure.* Telling her about myself is one thing, but telling her about Uriah, Rose, Mekaia; it's a whole other level.

"Please, Rowan. I want to know." My eyes meet hers and time stops; it's the first time she's said my name. *My actual name.* The way it sounds coming off her lips, I know I'm in deep shit. If I wasn't falling for her before, I definitely am now. Something as simple as that turned this conversation, and I would tell her everything about Heaven if I could remember it. I'd do anything for her, to her, and because of her.

"Our leader, Mekaia, was the first Fallen Angel. He retained his memory and is all knowing about us. He found me centuries ago, and-"

"Centuries? How old are you?" Is that seriously what she's focusing on right now?

"I've been on Earth for five hundred years. No telling how old I really am."

She shakes her head and pretends to be disgusted. "Don't you think it's weird for us to hang out like this? Doesn't that make you some kind of supernatural pervert?" I laugh loudly and throw my head back, she is something else. Uriah said he thought she had spunk, he doesn't even know the half of it. After laughing, we both get serious again. "Why were you kicked out?"

Mekaia's voice pops into my head and I let it out. "Love." She looks confused, of course she'd be. Why would love, something the Heavens preach about being so pure, get me kicked out for the rest of my lonely existence? "I loved someone, or so Mekaia says, and I broke the rules for her. This ended up getting me kicked out. Mekaia doesn't know what happened to her. And I can't remember it, so it's for the best." I can tell my explanation takes her by surprise. It's no doubt that we have been growing closer through this time together, and I hope she feels similar about me as I do her.

Right now, her raven hair is a mess, no doubt tangled from her fall off the building. She looks flushed, I'm sure that has something to do with almost dying and learning everything you thought you knew was wrong. The look of pain on her face doesn't go unnoticed, and in that moment, I'm snapped back to reality. "I shouldn't be telling you any of this." I stand up from the chair and maneuver my way towards the other side of the apartment. I hear the sound of soft footsteps behind me, and I should know better to think that she'll just let that go.

"Why? Doesn't this help our investigation? Won't it be nice to not have to keep secrets from me anymore?"

"I never wanted to keep them from you in the first place. But knowing all of this puts you, and myself, in so much danger." Just from what I know about her, I can tell she would go through Hell and back to stand her ground, she might be afraid but I don't think she'd ever back down from a fight.

"So what?"

"He could kill you, Samara." She places her hands on my chest and leans in closer to me, her whole body becomes flushed with mine, and for a split second I think that maybe, just maybe, this could work.

"I almost died tonight, Rowan." Our gazes match each other with a fiery, unspoken need. "You didn't let that happen. I'd bet money you won't let it happen again." She doesn't wait for my response before she continues, "You didn't have to save me tonight.

You could've let me splat against the concrete, but you didn't. You revealed yourself to me, and I'd like to think that you'd protect me too." She was right. I'd face Mekaia, Rose, Uriah and all the other fallen angels if I had to, just to keep her safe.

We are quiet for a minute, standing there in the dim light from the city, just looking into one another's eyes. She closes the distance and moves close enough where I can feel her breath fanning my skin. "Kiss me." My body complies with her demand before my mind does, and I wrap my hand around the back of her head and press our lips together. She's soft under my touch, and the warmth that explodes when our lips move is fresh in my mind. Especially when she doesn't pull away, and instead runs her arms up my body and around my neck, effectively locking me in place. A simple, innocent kiss, until she slides her tongue over my bottom lip, earning a groan from me.

My body's longing for a release and my mind's thoughts of her are enough to bring all my desires to the forefront as my other arm freely moves to her waist, pulling her closer to me. A soft moan escapes her lips and it takes everything in me not to escalate this further. I pull away, and a look of rejection appears on her face. "We still have a lot to talk about." She nods, agreeing and slowly removes her arms from around my neck. We walk back over to the bed, and this time, she makes room for me to sit with her.

The rest of the night is filled with more questions that I shouldn't be answering, and small laughs that escape whenever I say something she doesn't agree with. I tell her about the murderer, how they're supernatural, about how Mekaia put me in charge of finding them, and how I chose her to help. "So you just saw me at the first two and wanted to team up?" Her head is on my chest and one of my arms is wrapped around her, drawing her in close.

"You're a human. Two points of view could help us get to an answer quicker." I tell her about the legend of a perfect sacrifice, and how the murderer has to be a fallen angel. Explaining my history with Mekaia, Uriah, and most importantly Rose, which was the most uncomfortable topic of the night.

"So, let me get this straight." I become quiet, waiting for her to lay down the law, and she clears her throat before she starts speaking. "You are a literal angel who is hunting down a murderer of the same kind. You have sworn off love because that's why you got kicked out of Heaven, and hooked up with your boss' secretary. You've known about the black market this whole time and your contact at the police department has done nothing to stop it. To top it all off, you know about my date with Joshua, and you've been watching me from the building in front of my apartment."

Yeah, probably shouldn't have told her about any of this. "Yeah, looks like you got the gist of it." She chuckles slightly, and I think in her head she's excusing my possessiveness because she's realizing how much danger she was in. We are quiet for a long time afterwards, enjoying the closeness between us. I don't realize she is asleep until I say her name and get no response. Her breathing has relaxed, and for a second, she is taken away from all the chaos that has just now come into her world. Guilt pangs in my chest, I know I'm the cause of it, and that it's just the beginning.

TWENTY FIVE

Samara

I startle awake when Camille jumps onto the bed, and I realize that I'm back in my own apartment. Had last night been a dream? Had I truly not almost died? Or learned that Rowan was supernatural? Or kissed him? Camille must notice this look on my face because she starts speaking as soon as I look back at her. "Rowan brought you home early this morning. I've already called out of work for you, don't worry. You're safe."

Her voice is delicate and her face is still beautiful even with the bruises that litter her cheeks. She's close, ready to jump into action and hug me at any given time. Wait a second. "You called him Rowan. Did last night really happen?"

She nods slowly, slight fear showing on her face. "I was here whenever he brought you home, I practically threatened him with a butcher's knife to tell me what the hell happened." I chuckle, imagining Camille's short stature bowing up to Rowan's tall frame. "He told me everything. I'm so happy you're safe." She finally reaches in for that hug she's been longing for, and I return it with enthusiasm.

The tears start to streak my cheeks when I think about how she could've been alone. I'll make sure she's never alone, if it's the last thing I do. She pulls back first and grabs my shoulders with her hands. "Alright missy, you need to fill me in on everything. Now." Explaining everything to Camille was like telling a know-it-all the answers to the questions. Rowan told her about what happened at the club, and about who he is. He definitely omitted the kissing details, because when I told her that, she squealed loud enough to make me cover my ears. "You did what!?"

Her pride was stuck on her face when I told her I all but demanded Rowan to kiss me, and the smile that broke out on her face was worth it when I told her that he complied. "Oh my god, I bet he's such a good kisser." Hearing her swoon brings me back to her crush.

"Alright, now it's your turn. When am I going to meet this girlfriend of yours?" Her face turns blank and she replies quickly, "I don't know what you're talking about." She tries to get up from her spot on the bed, but I wrap my arms around her and pull her back down. "Oh no you don't."

She tells me all about the girl she likes. Her name is Jamie, she's a year older and they met in Camille's art class. She describes Jamie to me as an all american girl, blonde hair, green eyes, two parents and two siblings; she's the oldest. Apparently, that's who she was with whenever Rowan, Theo at the time, and I had our dinner. "Food was good, by the way." I smile, even being here for the past couple years, I still remember Momma's cooking. I should call her.

"If you didn't seal the deal with that kiss, maybe you did with your cooking."

"Well, if there's one thing you should know about Rowan, he doesn't do love."

She tilts her head at me. "But, that's what you're all about?"

I sucked a small breath in, "He didn't tell you, did he?" She shakes her head. Guess he omitted a couple more details.

"The reason he's here, on Earth, is because he fell in love."

Camille shakes her head, "That's not such a bad thing."

I shrug my shoulders and stand up, making my way to the bathroom. "Apparently in Heaven it is." I step into the bathroom and turn on the shower. I need to get rid of last night's events; well, not all of them. The warm water feels nothing like Rowan's body against me. I wash away the grimy feeling of Killian's hands on me, the lingering smell of sulfur, and the stuffy club air away. A clean canvas, a fresh start to the day.

With the events as of late, the days have started blending together. We don't have many leads on our investigation, and my job at Shapiro Informatics is still up in smoke. I take the time after my shower to write what I can of my report. I decided to title it: New York, New Age, New Killer. Although, knowing what I know now, I'm not sure this report will ever go live. How am I supposed to write this report on the supernatural? The actual killer will never be revealed, and who knows if Rowan and I can even find them? *Rowan.*

This has to be hard on him. Knowing that one of his own, one of the fallen angels, is responsible for these murders. From what he's told me about them, they are neither good nor evil. They rely on a certain amount of chaos in the world, and until the balance is broken, they won't step in. If Mekaia specifically told Rowan to find and take care of this perpetrator, then the balance must definitely be out of whack.

Camille is talking in the living room, assuming she's on the phone, I decide to go fix me something to eat. As soon as I open my door, Camille and another girl both jump up from the couch. I stop in my tracks, "Oh my gosh, I'm so sorry."

"Sam, this is Jamie."

Oh! "Jamie, it's nice to meet you. I've heard a lot about you." I walk up and give her a small hug.

She smiles when she pulls away. Of course I see what Camille see's in her. She's pretty and a little taller than Camille. Her blonde hair is falling in curls down her shoulders, her green eyes contrast well to Camille's brown ones.

"Same with you. Camille talks about you all the time."

I take pride in knowing how much Camille and I care about each other. The bond we've formed over these past couple years is something most people don't have the luxury of making their entire lives. I wonder if Rowan has anyone like this? Or ever has? "I was just about to make some food. Do you guys want any?"

Camille nods enthusiastically and Jamie chuckles at her response. "That would be great." I fixed us all up some toasted bagels with cream cheese. Camille and I take ours with bacon and Jamie just has hers plain. We talk for a little as we eat, then I excuse myself back to my room to give them some privacy. I take this time to finally give Momma a call, it's been a while since I've talked to her.

"Sammy! Hi honey." Her southern voice fills my ears and relief washes over me.

"Hi Momma. How are you?"

"Oh baby, don't worry about how I am. How are you? How's big city life?" I chuckle. Unlike most people, my momma was so supportive of my move to New York City. Her and Dad always knew I was destined for big things, and they had been saving up to help me through everything: high school, college, and even my move up here.

"Big city life isn't always what it's cut out to be. But I'm doing alright. I miss you Momma."

I hear her chuckle. "You'll be alright, honey. I miss you more, are you sure everything's okay?"

I start to sniffle but I hold it in. I can't tell her about almost dying or how I'm surrounded by supernatural creatures at every turn. "Yeah Momma, I'm alright." I decide to tell her about Rowan, but not the details. She's always ready to hear any boy crazy stories, she doesn't get them from me very often. "I actually wanted to tell you about this boy I met, his name is Rowan."

"Rowan, oh he sounds sexy. I want to hear all about him."

I throw my head back and laugh, "Momma, please!" I hear her chuckle on the other end.

"Well you know I worry about you, Sammy." Momma knows that I take care of Camille, but she's always asking if there's anyone to take care of me.

"I think you'd like him." I go on to tell her all the details about our dinner and first kiss. I can feel her blushing over the phone.

"That hamburger steak always does it. How do you think I got your father so fast?" I chuckle. We don't talk about Dad that much, but he's always there with us. Now that I know Heaven and Hell are real, I hope he's up there. "Alright honey, I've got to go.

I'm going out to dinner with the girls. Call me later?" I smile knowing that even though I'm here, she's got people back home to be there with her. "I love you, Sammy." I smile, the amount that I miss her increasing by the second.

"I love you too, Momma. Call you soon."

TWENTY SIX

Rowan

After dropping Samara off back at her apartment, and being faced with a furious Camille brandishing a butcher knife, I need to go see Mekaia and tell him what's happened. I've already told Samara, so it's a case of asking for forgiveness rather than permission. As I come through the doors of his office, I'm met with a hand to the throat.

"You told me you'd never do such treason and here you are! Blabbing our secrets to a filthy human!" What surprises me is that Rose is the one to deliver the blow.

"So what, I wasn't good enough to be with, to trust, but she is?" Mekaia is giving me daggers from over her shoulder, and then I see a guilty looking Uriah.

"Maybe you should ask Uriah what happened, he's the one who showed his wings first." Rose's eyes look like they're glowing with rage, she whips her head over and stares Uriah down.

"You must have omitted that detail." When Rose is angry, nothing can stand in her path. She's so close to Mekaia for a reason; her and Uriah are some of our best assets and strongest warriors.

"Dude, you said if things go sideways to get out of there! How was I supposed to know that you would stay and save the girl?"

"I basically laid it out on a platter-"

Mekaia stands, knocking his chair back in the process. "Enough!" The room goes silent, besides our heavy breathing. It's not unknown that Mekaia is hanging on by a thread, all of us scared for how he will react, no sudden movements. Rose releases my throat, unhappily, and stands away with her head down.

"Everyone but Rowan, get the hell out." Rose and Uriah swiftly move out of the office and when it's just Mekaia and I, he picks his chair back up and sits down. "Rowan, what do you expect me to do?"

I walk closer to the front of his desk. "Let me explain." Mekaia's eyes have turned red, but he nods and motions for me to go ahead.

"Samara is the reporter that I have been teaming up with to find more leads on this investigation. You wanted me to find the murderer, and that's exactly what I'm doing."

"I never told you to tell a human our secrets. It's treason." I nod, realizing how difficult this situation has become. The feeling of Samara's touch was definitely a factor in me letting my fat lips loose.

"I realize that and I take responsibility for my actions. But not only was it the only way to keep her alive, it's also the only way for us to get the answers that we need."

He nods and is quiet for a moment. "Rose isn't happy."

A small light hearted comment eases the tension in the room. "I don't think she'll ever be happy again."

He smiles softly. "How many others know?"

"A couple drunk partiers and Samara's roommate, Camille."

He scoffs and I finish his thought before he can get it out, "Those are the only two who will know. They're a package deal. She threatened me with a butcher's knife. I think you'd like her."

He chuckles slightly, "Anything else I have to scold you for?"

"I think I'm falling for her." The room is so quiet I can hear my heartbeat. There aren't many rules for us here, if any at all. But I'm not sure if doing the same thing you got kicked out of Heaven for crosses a line.

Mekaia sees my internal struggle and sighs, "Rowan, I've always looked at you as a son and I trust you with my life." With this declaration, I feel like whatever falls after can't be good. "There's something you should know."

He stands from his desk and walks to a shelf that's to my left. He grabs an old, leather book and walks back towards his desk, standing beside me. Once he opens it, he slips through the pages quickly and lands on an excerpt with a picture of an angel falling to Earth, their wings in the process of turning black. The excerpt is titled Deja Vu, and is pretty short for a book of this stature. "Read it." He walks back to his seat as I begin to read.

"Fallen angels are cast out when commands are disobeyed, as is the cause of the disobeyment. The fallen retain their gift of immortality as a punishment on Earth, but their cause is given a life of a doppelganger. Forced to live away from part of their soul. The lifetimes will bring the two parts of one soul together again, but in agony, the same consequences will happen."

I look up to meet Mekaia's normal eyes, and they're filled with unshed tears. He clears his throat, "I always told you that your reason for being cast out was love; turns out, that's everyone's reason." A punch to the gut is the best way to describe what I'm feeling right now. "Love for another, love for themselves, love for the innocent. It all resorts back to love." I shake my head and look closer to the page, the angel in the picture resembles Mekaia, and it all comes together.

"You wrote the archives." He nods and looks down at the book.

"Until more of you fell, I had to write our history." I shake my head and lean against his desk with my hands.

"But what does this mean exactly?" I point to the page with one of my hands and he sighs, sadly.

"What it's saying is, whoever had the direction of your love is cast down and forced to live the same as you."

"I don't understand."

He stands and moves from behind the desk, walking up to me and putting his hands on my shoulders. "The pull you feel from Samara, is the same pull you felt for her in Heaven." No. She was there? Is she a fallen angel too? Why doesn't she have powers? "The angel is cast down and set to live our life, but the recipient of the love is cast down as a human doppelganger."

I push his arms off of me. "So you're saying that Samara has lived six, maybe seven lifetimes, all to find me once again?"

He nods, "All five hundred years you've been down here, Samara's soul has been down here, searching for you." The news slaps me across the face. I could've met her sooner?

"It says it's a punishment, what does that mean?"

He sits against his desk. "We are immortal, forever. They are not. We are forced to be without them, find them, love them, and then watch them die."

No way. I wouldn't let anything happen to Samara, let alone her dying. I've never met her before in all my years, why would that be our fate the first time? "So, she's the one I loved in Heaven?" Mekaia looks sad, he's probably remembering his time, his love, in Heaven.

"An exact replica. Actually half of your soul, the one who makes you complete." This information frightens me, but also makes sense. I never truly had to swear off love because someone else had my heart the entire time.

"Can I tell her this?" I feel like my legs may collapse, the breath my lungs shallow and nonexistent.

"You can if you choose. If you tell her, though, I can't guarantee she will come back for another life." What? "I've been through it."

Again, what? "I found my love three times in my life. The last time, I told them about the Deja Vu rule and I haven't found them since." Now, I can't tell her. I can't risk finding her and never having her again.

I sigh and run my hands through my hair, "Thank you, for sharing this Mekaia."

"I love you like a son, Rowan. Just be careful."

TWENTY SEVEN

Samara

Five people from my floor at Shapiro Informatics have been let go in just the past couple days. The pressure is officially on. "Sam, can we talk?" If only Joshua was one of those people.

"Joshua, if you ever mutter a single word to her again, I will castrate you." Francis comes behind me and says exactly what comes to mind, no doubt having hard feelings for when I filled her in.

"I want to talk to Sam, not you."

"Well, I don't want to talk to you. I said everything I needed to." I can feel his presence leave us. "Thank you, Francis."

"No need to thank me. I've been wanting to tell him off for a long time."

I start typing on my computer and pull up the article that I've started on. "Did you have a chance to read it?" Francis moves from behind me and leans up against the barrier or my cubicle.

"Yeah, I left my annotations in the document online." I feel her gaze shift from the computer to me. "Sam?" I stop typing and look at her. She looks tired, the bags under her green eyes highlight that.

"Francis, are you okay?"

She shakes her head, "I could ask you the same thing."

I keep a small mirror in my cubicle, mostly to fix my makeup in case a story happens, I turn to look at it and see I share the same bags under my eyes. "You called out sick, you don't look good, and after everything that happened with Joshua-"

"Nothing happened with Joshua." I correct her, we kissed but that was it, thank God. I take this time to look in the mirror and she's right, I don't look so good. Truthfully, it's to be expected after the days I've had.

"You looked so drained. Maybe it's best if you go home." Going home and laying in my bed, doing absolutely nothing sounds like exactly what I need right now. Although, I'm scared what Ms. Shapiro will think when it's my time for an evaluation. "I'll put in a good word for you, don't worry." Francis reads my mind and helps me gather my things. I figure it's for the best. This way, I'll be able to work on my article if I get any more ideas, but I'll also be able to have appropriate rest.

When I get home, Camille isn't there. She's probably out with some friends from school, and maybe even spending some alone time with Jamie. My heart flutters thinking about how happy Camille seems. She told me that she's sworn off her father, he's messed up too many times to remedy any of it. I can't say that I wouldn't do the same thing, especially after Rowan and I had to pick her off her father's floor. Her bruises have almost completely disappeared, I can only imagine the kind of questions she was getting when they were fresh.

I decide to directly change into some loose fitting pajamas and lay down. The rainy day probably also directly affects my mood, but it makes for a great sound to fall asleep to. I watch the droplets race down my window, secretly praying for the smaller one to cross the finish line first. I focus my eyes on the building directly in front of mine, and look to the roof. Rowan told me that's where he watched me from. At first, it was creepy; the kind of creepy when someone finds all your social media after saying "Hello," one time. But, when he told me more about his world, and I quickly realized I was getting wrapped up in it without even knowing, I was all for a little more protection than Camille with a butcher's knife. I wonder if he's there, watching me now?

I decide to text him, surely a centuries old supernatural creature knows how to text. I mean, he was there when it was invented.

Samara: Hey, what's up?

I wait a couple moments, and I get no reply. He's probably busy being the police of the supernatural world. I reach for my laptop and open it, ready to start on a bit of my report, when my phone buzzes.

Rowan: Nm

Bland. A boring man. That's the first thing that pops into my head when he responds. I feel like a bother now that I've seen how he responds.

Rowan: Sorry, don't text much.

Huh, phone calls and in person visits I guess. That fits him more than texting. I know it may be stepping over a line to ask him to come over, just to hangout. But, as I'd tell him, we would continue working on our investigation.

Rowan: Home today?

Oh boy, I don't know if he knows the multiple text rules, but he's looking a little desperate right now. The question makes me think, once again, if he's watching me from across the street. Through the rain that has now turned into just a drizzle, I look to the roof and through what light leaks through the clouds; I see a figure. Whether it's him or not, I don't know. Finding out about the supernatural world has me in a whirlwind. There could be many people after me now that I know the history of the fallen angels.

Samara: Yeah, you?
Rowan: Yeah

Is that not him across the street? I look back where the figure was and black wings stretch out from them as they are hoisted into the sky. I waste no time in calling Rowan, screw this texting shit, I need to talk to him. "Samara?"

"Rowan, don't lie, was that you across the street just now?" It should be answer enough that it's silent over the phone, besides his clothes shuffling.

"I'm at my apartment. Is someone there?"

My breath hitches in my throat when I hear my doorbell ring. "I think they're at my door."

Rowan's voice comes out frantic but powerful, "Samara, do not move! I am on the way."

He hangs up before I can protest, and I know he will be here as fast as his wings can carry him. I, however, do not want to sit here waiting for the end. I quietly open my bedroom door, which seems useless when I remember many supernatural creatures have super hearing. Although, they also have supernatural strength, so why waste the time ringing my doorbell? Why not just crash through and kill me? Creeping into the kitchen, which, again, feels very human, I grab the biggest knife from the block and hold it confidently. I try not to laugh when I remember this is the same way Camille threatened Rowan when he brought me home that night.

A bang against my door makes me jump, and the knife falls through my fingers. My heart feels like it'll give out, but I'd take that over being killed by whatever is behind my door. It's quiet once again, so I pick it back up and slowly start walking towards the door. When close enough to feel my breath fanning back onto me, I look into the peephole to see what, or who, it is.

Whoever is out there, is wearing a black hoodie and a mask, I can't see a single part of their face. But that's not what worries me the most, or even what scares me. What frightens me is the fact that whoever this is has their wings out in the middle of the hallway. They look bigger than Rowan's, but their feathers are thinning and the color is fading into a dark gray. The first thing that comes into my mind is the question of: is this the killer? Is this flimsy door the only thing separating me from a psycho who doesn't care about anyone?

We are both leaning so close to the door, being able to hear each other's breath. Their head snaps up and all I can see are their blood red eyes. "*Samara.*" They say my name and it makes me want to vomit. It doesn't sound like how Rowan says it, they sound like they're mocking it. "I know who you are." My blood runs cold. Their voice sounds so demonic, I can't even tell if it's a man or a woman. "See you soon." Is the last thing they say before they vanish into seemingly thin air. My breathing is hard and when Rowan pops into my line of vision, I scream.

"Samara?" His voice saying my name makes my eyes tear up. I'm not sure about everything with our connection, but I know I feel peace when I'm with him. He yanks the door open and grabs me into a hug, I feel his heart beating out of his chest, mirroring my own. His arm is wrapped around my waist and his other hand is holding my head against his chest. His hand is almost the size of my whole head. "I'm sorry I didn't get here faster. What happened?" I tell Rowan all about the mysterious Fallen Angel outside my door, what they said and specifics on how they look.

"It seems like they're truly too far gone." It saddens me to know that someone can live an immortal life that they didn't choose, and then have to live through going crazy.

"Are you sure they had red eyes?" I nod, his question must have meaning because he's quiet for a minute, staring off into the distance. "The fact that they were showing their wings in such a public space is a red flag. Our wings are our most prized possession, if we didn't have to show anyone, I don't think we would." This peaks interest in me. I remember seeing Uriah's, but I guess that was a life or death situation, and to be fair it happened so fast. But Rowan's, he's carried me before with them, but I don't think I've ever seen them up close.

Before I know it the words are spilling out of my mouth, "Can I see yours?"

TWENTY EIGHT

Rowan

She has no idea what she's saying. To see our wings, it's the most intimate part of us. It's more intimate than sex. I feel the heat running up my face and I clear my throat, definitely taken aback by her question. She catches on to this and asks, "What's so wrong with the question?"

I shake my head and decide to give her a taste of her own medicine. "Nothing's wrong, Samara. I mean, I should be thrilled, you basically just asked me for sex." I can see the whites of her eyes grow larger and I suppress my laugh until she stays nothing; she just stands there with her mouth agape, looking like a deer in headlights.

"Samara, I'm kidding." She closes her mouth and reaches to punch me, but I dodge and grab her arm, twisting her around so her back is pressed against me.

"What I mean to say, is that asking to see my wings," I lean down closer, letting her warmth spread and allowing my mouth to touch her ear as I finish the thought. "Is the most intimate thing someone like me can participate in."

I feel her shiver throughout my whole body, it delights me to know I can make her feel this way. I wish I could make her more comfortable with our connection by telling her about Deja Vu, but I can't risk never having her again. To never love her again is to have my wings burned off of me, slow but fast and painful all the time. I let her go so she can face me once again.

"I understand if you don't want-"

"If you still want to, I am more than happy to oblige." I cut her off, she's the only person I want to show anything to. She nods slowly, her cheeks becoming a rose color. That darkens when I start removing my clothes.

"What are you doing?" The comment from earlier fresh in her mind, she holds out a hand and backs up slightly.

"Samara, my dear, my wings are eight feet long, they will rip my shirt to shreds, and for your sake I would like to have something to cover myself with after the fact."

She's the one who demanded a kiss from me, and now she's the one who wants to see my wings. She is the one we should be worrying about. She closes her mouth and I get no more protests from her throughout the experience. We are both quiet and our movements are slow, both of us lost in the thought of being so close to one another.

When my shirt is off, I take a look at her and my wings start to spread from my body. The quiet cracking of my bones and the 'woosh' of my wings once they spread. Her eyes turn from embarrassment to awe as she gazes at them. The fallen angels have a certain level of animal instincts, we're predators, and seeing her in awe of my wings makes me proud. I stand higher, making myself taller than I already am, and it all comes crumbling down when she begins to walk around me. A pit in my gut feels like it's going to explode, and I try my best to keep the inappropriate thoughts at bay.

That goes to shit whenever she reaches out and touches them. A fluttering touch from her fingertips all but makes me moan. A harsh breath leaves my lungs and I feel her fingers retreat for a moment.

I can only imagine the thoughts in her head.

My skin prickles with anticipation knowing she's this close to me, the coldness sticking to my skin since she pulled back. I think about it for a second and realize, I crave her touch too much to go without it. I take a minimal step back towards her hand, allowing her whole palm to touch between my shoulder blades, between my wings.

This time, I moan, because she runs her hand down my back and slightly scratches with the tip of her fingernails. Raw and guttural is what it sounds like on my end, and I hope I didn't just embarrass myself in front of her.

I can't see her, I can just feel her presence behind me, moving agonizingly slow. She walks towards the ends of my feathers, and gentle rubs. Right now she's feeling bone with a feather cover, a literal extension of my body. I wonder what she's thinking, and I'm fighting tooth and nail to not ask her to say something. When she makes her way around the front of my wings until she is facing me, she stares deeply into my eyes. The last time I saw this look on her face was when she demanded to kiss me. It's something mixed between awe, determination, fear, and want. She brings one of her hands to my chest and uses the other to cup one side of my face. I close my eyes and lean into her warmth as far as I can go, wishing it could be like this forever.

"You are beautiful." Her voice snaps my eyes open. I'm not sure how to react, I know it's a compliment, but I've never had one that meaningful before. Sure, adjectives like: sexy, hot, irresistible were thrown around here and there, but never *beautiful*. It's like a foreign word she could repeat a million times and I still wouldn't get it. My mouth just sits in a thin line and she isn't sure what to do. It doesn't take her long to decide when she pulls my head down to meet her lips at full force.

Both of us surrender to the tension in the air, she jumps and simultaneously I wrap my arms under her and hold her around my own waist. Both of us aren't able to ignore the elephant in the room, or more like the one between my legs. I walk us over to her bed and lay her down gently, her legs never shift from around my waist, I duck from our heated kiss to leave a trail of them down her neck and her collarbone.

She lets out a breathy moan and moves her hips a little. That's the game, the one where I lose and pull my wings back into my body, ready to take this further. "Freaky." She mutters playfully and I stop kissing her to hover my face above hers.

"Yeah? Let's see how much freakier I can get." I return to kissing her, worshiping every part of her body I can with those dreadful clothes on.

She pushes me away to take off her shirt, her movements intoxicating. Her small frame lies perfectly underneath me. Her bra is still on and I waste no time moving the straps to the side to plant wet kisses all along her body. I move through her valley, down her stomach, and to the waistline of her shorts. I look up, pleading with my eyes, and ask her, "What do you want?" Her breathing is hard and she's looking at her ceiling, not at me. This hurts my pride.

I've got you under me, wanting to pleasure you, and you aren't even looking at me? "Samara," I finally captured her attention with the use of her name. "What do you want?"

"I want you." Her response seals our fate as I loop my fingers through her shorts and pull them down. Stupid clothes, didn't need you anyways. As she lay under me, almost completely bare, I sit up on my knees and take her in.

She's the most beautiful girl that I've ever seen.

I'd see her beauty anywhere in the world. It's the same beauty that you see when droplets fall off leaves after a heavy rain. It's the same beauty in the song the birds sing. The same beauty of dawn and dusk, the beginning and the end. I actually pray to God in that one moment to always have her and her beauty with me. When I'm done admiring her–which will never truly be over–I begin to leave kisses up her legs, the end in sight.

She squirms and releases breathy moans-adding fuel to the fire is more like it. Once I reach her center, blowing softly on it to make her hips buckle, I lay my tongue flat against her. I taste and drink her up, her need flowing smoothly. Her hands find my hair and she wraps it around her fingers, tugging occasionally. I feel myself pressing tightly against my jeans, painfully aware of the aching that's started. I can't take it too fast, it's been a while since I've had sex, and I'm sure it's been a while for her too.

My mind flashes back to that date she had, just for a moment, I think to myself, *'He couldn't have handled her anyways.'*

I continue to pleasure her, just to hear her voice in ways no one else can, to see her body contort with need whenever I change paces or move over.

"*Rowan*," If she keeps talking, I'll probably finish before we even get to the good part. "Get up here."

Yes ma'am. I'd love to finish feasting on her, but she doesn't have to tell me twice before I am up and pressed flush against her. Her hands move frantically towards my pants, trying to unbutton them but struggling. I hold her hands, stopping them from shaking. "Samara, do you want to do this?" She visibly rolls her eyes. She takes me by surprise and throws my weight to the side, now on top of me. The way she looks and moves I want nothing more than to plunge into her, but knowing Samara, that's not how this will go at all.

"Shut up." She mutters before she unbuttons my pants and pulls my dick out. The feeling of her hand on my bare extremity has me fisting a section of her bedsheets and breathing hard, trying not to finish already. My horny brain urges me to grab her hips and sink her down onto me, but I'm perfectly content when she slides her tongue up my shaft. I groan and wrap my hands in her hair, letting her bob her head to her heart's content. Whatever and however she wants it, she sets the speed, she's in control.

When she's had enough, she goes and moves her waist upwards, closer to mine. I don't want our first time to be with her on top. She needs to be shown what it's like to be a queen. Just as she did before me,

I flip us over so I'm on top of her. She wraps her legs around my waist but stops me before we go further.

"Condom." Responsible, I love her more and more every day. I lean closer to her neck and whisper, my breath fanning her sensitive skin. "I can't have kids, and I also can't get diseases." She smiles and nods so I begin to push into her, slowly but surely.

I think just by the moan that leaves her throat and the way she squeezes me that I'll finish right then and there. She wraps her arms around me and pulls me closer, the feeling of her bra on my chest aggravates me, and I remove it as fast as I can. "Rowan, you aren't moving?"

I chuckle but quickly stop, the movement reverberating through me. "I want to make sure you enjoy it." I start to slide out and push back in, dreadfully slow. Her nails scratch into my back, and I almost stop because I think that maybe she can't handle this right now. It isn't until she begins to moan and move her hips on her own, meeting mine with every thrust that I begin to speed up. Sweat beads line our foreheads as we exchange sloppy kisses, both caught up in the feeling of the closeness with each other. The lustful pang in my stomach is growing, burning for her. I can tell she's close, and I'll be damned for eternity if I don't see unravel under me. A little while longer and she tightens around me, crying out and putting her head in the crook of my neck. It doesn't take me long to finish after her, holding myself steady as I plant a kiss on her lips, claiming her as mine.

I roll off of her and face the city buildings as she turns to me, cuddling up against my chest. I could get used to this. After a few moments of heavy breathing, she looks up at me and just stares. "What?"

She shakes her head, avoiding my question. "I can't answer right now." I chuckle and pull her closer as we move under the covers. She falls asleep soon after, the sound of gentle rain against the windows.

"I love you." I whisper quietly, so I know she won't wake up. Looking back over to the city, I decide to drift asleep, but not before I see the silhouette across the street. Black wings out, facing directly into the room. I can't leave to chase them now, I won't leave her alone after our time together.

I just hope they enjoyed the show.

TWENTY NINE

Samara

I wake up in a warm embrace and try to go further into it. Knowing the world is completely different from this silence, I never want to leave. "Samara," Oh, his voice. The drunk feeling of making love still fresh in my brain, and body, I flutter my eyes open to see him looking down at me. "I would say good morning, but it's the middle of the night."

Brother, I will never get this sleeping schedule right again.

"Hi," My voice is small but raspy, past activities catching up with my body's endurance.

"Hey yourself. I'm about to order some food, what do you want?"

We decide on chinese and I guess by the way I hear mumbling in the den that Camille is home. Great, having her see Rowan walking out with no shirt on is exactly what her perverted teenager mind needs. While waiting for Rowan to call and order the food, which is just funny knowing he's an immortal being, Camille barges through the door. I squeal and pull the covers as far up as they can go because I am still naked. "Shut the fuck up!"

"Camille! Language!"

She laughs and jumps on the end of the bed at my feet. "Did you do that thing?" I stare at her blankly, I should not be telling her about this. She's sixteen for christ sakes, she doesn't need to know.

"Maybe." We both squeal and a concerned Rowan comes through the door.

"What?"

Camille puts her hands over her mouth and my mouth just hangs open, admiring him. He looks like he works out everyday, no doubt you have to be strong to carry those wings around; it could also be a supernatural blessing kind-of-thing.

"We're okay." I finally say and he nods and turns around, going back into the den and shutting the door behind him. "Camille, frankly you are too young to know the details of my sex life and to be in bed while I am naked!"

She jumps off the bed in a hurry. "It happened right here, right here?" She stands awkwardly and points to a spot on the bed.

"Yes Camille. It happened in the bed. Right here, right here." Without saying another word she just begins to dust off her pants and walk out of the room. I laugh as I can hear her and Rowan fussing in the kitchen.

I get out of bed, shakily, and make my way to the shower. Desperately needing to wash off and get ready for the next adventure, I hear Rowan click open the door and move the shower curtain. "Oh no, buddy boy. This is completely different from what we did last night." He chuckles but steps in anyway, ignoring my protests. He grabs my shampoo and puts a decent amount in the center of his palm. He's standing in front of me, rubbing his hands together to mix the shampoo. He motions his head for me to turn around, to which I oblige; the shower water hitting the front of my chest. I try to maintain eye contact as I turn around, not wanting to look at the member below me.

"In olden times," Rowan starts telling me a story as he rubs his fingers through my hair, effectively washing it for me. I close my eyes and listen to his voice. "Some of the fallen began to adjust quickly to life down here. They would marry."

This strikes some surprise in me, they're immortal, would they get married to one another?

"Knowing about their immortal nature, they would pick another fallen to share their existence with. It would be less lonely this way." On any given day, I'm lonely and I only have Camille and Francis, now Rowan. I'm not sure what I'd do if I had no one. "Their wedding ceremonies would be different from regular human ones. The man would wash his betrotheds hair, to show her that he can take care of her."

"What would the woman do?" By now, he's rinsed my hair and has started on the conditioner, but I see what he's doing. He likes to get me flustered, and talking about marriage and what they do at their wedding ceremonies is a good way to achieve that.

"The woman would wash the feet of her betrothed, to show the same thing. They do these actions for one another to prove that through the hard times of eternity, they would be able to provide, care, and defend each other."

Be bold, I think to myself. I move Rowan's hands out of my hair, and switch spots with him, so now his back is facing the water. I turn and look into his blue eyes, they're dark and a small smile creeps on his lips. I think he knows what I'm planning before I do. I mirror his past movements, putting soap in my hand and I get on my knees to crouch down. I tap his left leg and he lifts it up, letting me run my hands to wash his foot.

It's kinda weird, I definitely feel that. But with the story he told me and the actions he did, it's only fair that I do the same, and I want to. I repeat the same process with the other foot, and I glance up to look at him. His frame is intimidating as the light above the shower blocks out his face, and for a second, I'm afraid. I snap out of it when I feel his arms under mine, lifting me off the floor with no struggle, and plants me back on my feet in front of him. We stare into each other's eyes for a couple moments. Relishing the fact that, with a little less details, we just had a marriage ceremony. Our actions, our bodies and our eyes say everything that both of us are too scared to say out loud. He reaches down to kiss me, searching my mouth with his tongue. It gets heated in no time, he's moving his hands over my water covered waist and is leaving kisses on my chest. Dipping his head lower to go towards my nipple, he takes it in his mouth, warmth engulfing it before he moves it between his teeth, nibbling.

A small moan leaves my mouth that's quickly interrupted when we jump from banging on the door. "Food is here!" Camille's voice floods the room and we both chuckle and get out of the shower. I find some clothes for Rowan and we both change into something more relaxing. Camille is doing schoolwork, so Rowan and I come back to my room to eat. We sit in silence for a little bit, enjoying the food and each other's company. I can tell Rowan wants to say something, I won't push him, but the small movements he makes move him closer and the way his eyes linger on my actions for an extended time give him away. "Rowan," He shifts uncomfortably.

"Yes?"

I put my food down and stare at him for a second. "You have been staring at me this whole time. What do you want to say?"

Rowan doesn't hesitate now that I've brought it up, "I think you should meet Mekaia." My breath gets caught in my throat and a pit in my stomach begins to grow.

"You want me, your human girlfriend, to meet your immortal fallen angel leader after he knows you weren't supposed to tell me about yourself?" He nods, oblivious to how frightening this could be for me. I've seen their wings, I know they're immortal, I haven't seen their strength all the way but if Rowan could lift Killian off the ground and fly with me in his arms, I don't doubt the pain they could cause me if they wanted to. "How do you know he won't hurt me?"

"Let's just say that Mekaia and I had a heart to heart. Besides," He leans in close and cups my face with his hand. "I would rather die than let anyone hurt you." I trust Rowan, but that doesn't mean I'm not nervous about it. He doesn't smile and his mouth is in a straight line. I'd be foolish if I didn't catch onto it.

"You want this for the investigation." He nods slightly, here we go again. Last time I was involved with something for this investigation, I was thrown off a building. To be fair, that was of my own volition, but still, I almost died.

"I don't trust Mekaia as much." Mekaia was the leader and Rowan is second in command, trust is most of their relationship: what happens when that trust dissipates?

"You described the person who was here with blood red eyes." I nod and wait for his explanation. "I've told you when fallen angels spend too long away from Heaven they slowly go insane. During that process, their eyes can turn red." Cool, now it's a psychotic fallen angel that's after me and murdering all these people. "Mekaia's eyes have been turning red lately." Great, now it's the leader of the fallen angels. This conversation just keeps getting better.

"So it's Mekaia that's after me and murdering these people? But why? There doesn't seem to be anything he could gain from it.."

"Maybe, but if it is him, he thinks there is something he can get out of it."

"Well? What is it?" Rowan sighs and pulls me from my spot beside him to sit in front of him, careful not to turn over our food.

"There's something I need to tell you." The familiar pit in my stomach surfaces and it takes everything in me not to run. When Rowan goes in slow on a topic, it's really bad, I've come to learn that quickly. "There's a legend, or a myth if you will, that a perfect sacrifice can get a fallen angel back into Heaven."

I stare blankly for a minute. "Myth? perfect sacrifice?" He places a finger on my lips, effectively silencing me, making me listen.

"It's a myth because it's never worked. It's in our history books and many fallen have tried. None of them ever succeeded."

"What is a perfect sacrifice?"

Rowan shrugs. "Your guess is as good as mine. Like I said, no one has ever gotten back in, so it's obviously not whatever they're doing."

"What does this have to do with Mekaia and the murders?"

"When we met at the coffee shop that day for the first time, and you mentioned that the murderer was building a doll, I remembered the myth."

Ha, I'm too smart for my own good.

"This person is clearly killing people for their body parts. He's building a body, a perfect body for a perfect sacrifice. He wants entry back into Heaven." I nod, it's sad to know these people died for possibly nothing. If nothing has ever worked, what makes Mekaia think that this will?

"So, what does this have to do with me?"

Rowan shakes his head and stands up from me quickly. "I can't tell you." Huh?

"Why not exactly? You're the one that wants me to meet him."

"I want you to meet a couple of fallen angels that are around Mekaia, and then Mekaia himself. This is going to let me be able to figure out who is the killer. They'll all be so focused on you they won't keep track of me observing them." I shake my head, the nervousness turning to nausea. He crouches in front of me, propping his arms on my legs and clasping his hands together: praying. "Samara," Our eyes connect and the world stops. "I will never ask anything of you ever again. Please, do this for me."

THIRTY

Rowan

It only took half an hour of groveling before Samara actually agreed to what I was proposing. I know she's nervous, and I wish there was a way for me to explain to her that when I say nothing will happen to her, I mean it. I guess catching her from falling off a building isn't good enough. I change into my clothes from earlier and while Samara gets dressed. I'm not sure what she tells Camille when we're leaving, but Camille looks afraid for just a minute before she looks at me and says, "Protect her with your life." She doesn't even know half of it.

There's no way for a human to kill a fallen angel, but if there were it would be the death glare I am getting from Samara after asking her to jump in my arms so I can fly us there. After a slightly tiring battle of continuous "No!" and "Yes!", she finally gives in.

"Trust me." I say as I cup her face and stare into her eyes. She closes her eyes, reveling in the fact that our skin is touching. To me, the flight to Mekaia's office was normal, but to Samara, she was probably going through all five stages of grief. Landing on my feet, her in my arms, she holds on so tightly; gripping my shirt as hard as she can until I feel her breathing begin to slow.

She grabs my hand, insisting on touching me at least some way throughout this process. As we make our way through the abandoned building to his office, she gets as close to me as possible. It's like her nervousness is rubbing off on me, because the nauseous pang is making my stomach twitch. When that hits, I start to doubt if this was as good of an idea as I originally thought. "Rowan?" I hear Samara's small voice bring me out of my daze, to lock eyes with a furious Rose.

"What the hell is she doing here?" Rose stalks up to Samara and I step in front of her, protectively. "What little miss priss can't take care of herself?" Despite the fact that Rose choked me out not too long ago, I don't think I've ever seen her this mad or disgusted at a human. Well, Samara is my human, so she's going to learn to back the fuck off.

Before I can even answer her and defend Samara, she speaks for me. "Rowan brought me here. Is there an issue?" I can tell she's trying not to let her nerves get the better of her, and she's trying to hold her own.

"It is when I don't want you here."

"Oh for Hell's sake Rose, don't make me pull the authority shit." I huff at Rose quickly before Samara can respond. I appreciate her trying to hold her own, but she shouldn't have to, not with me around.

"Whatever." She mumbles as she turns around to go to her desk. I grab Samara's hand and lead her to Mekaia's doors.

"Are you ready?" She nods slowly, looking up to meet my eyes. Before she responds she looks behind us to stare Rose down. I see a small smirk play on her lips before she leans her head against my arm and kisses it. I take no time in following suit as I kiss the top of her head.

If Rose could catch fire, she'd be burning the whole place down. I can practically feel the anger rolling off her like a tsunami. Samara's a little devil if I've ever seen one, I realize that poking the dragon may have not been the best idea, but it's funny seeing Samara jealous and Rose angry. I could make this a good pastime of mine. I knock on the door and wait for his response to come through. "Enter." Oh no, he's in a bad mood before we even come inside. I pull Samara to go behind me, no doubt she's peeking around my frame to see what's going on. "Rowan, I see you've brought your friend."

"Mekaia, this is Samara." I step to the side, allowing him to gaze upon her without distractions. Maybe that was a bad decision, because now I'm jealous. Samara looks amazing right now, her hair slowly drying, forming slow curls. Mekaia wastes no time in rushing in front of her, slightly startling me, and taking a strand of her hair between his fingers. The look on Samara's face is a mixture of pain and shock. I want to move, but I don't know if it will set off Mekaia; he may be more animalistic than normal. A beautiful girl who is obviously afraid sat right in front of him? It's like asking for a chase. "Samara, what a beautiful name." She relaxes a little bit as he continues talking, and he meticulously backs away from her. "Rowan has told me so much about you." He sits back down at his desk, and we return to standing in front of him, hand in hand. "What brings you two here, other than pissing Rose off?"

I chuckle and the tension in the air is slowly falling away. I rub circles on Samara's hand to comfort her. "We have found out a little bit more about the murders, and have an idea about why they're happening." It doesn't shock Mekaia when we tell him about the killer wanting to complete a perfect sacrifice.

"It's been done countless times in my lifetime. I haven't known anyone to try in the last decade though." Then, Mekaia tells us something that sends shockwaves through us. "Rowan, I want you to take Samara to the library." This puzzles her but means something completely different for me.

"Library?"

"Are you sure?" Samara and I both talk at the same time.

To her, this means we are going to read books. To me, this means Mekaia has accepted her as my, whatever we are, and gives her permission to learn more about us. "Consider it a gift."

I nod my head to Mekaia, showing my respect. "Thank you."

He nods, "Dismissed."

Samara lowers her head slightly and mumbles, "Good to meet you." Before we are out of his office and passing Rose once more.

A small smile graces Rose's lips, paired with a light wave. "See you later, Samara."

THIRTY ONE

Samara

That Rose girl gives me the creeps. I'm not sure if it's because of the way she says my name, like it's poison on her tongue, or if it's the fact that she used to sleep with Rowan. I couldn't help the jealousy that flooded my veins, sometimes you just have to show a girl who's boss. By now, Rowan and I are in the library, apparently this library holds all supernatural documents and there are several throughout the world. The stained glass roof along with the sculptures that litter the area make me feel like I'm frozen in time. Back to a time where this was what every library looked like. I'm overwhelmed with the amount of information here.

Rowan starts showing me around and showing me which books pertain to which creature. "Here we have demons, like Killian." I shiver at the memory, I wonder what that demon is up to? "Werewolves, vampires, ah, fallen angels." We turn a corner and the books here are old, wrinkled leather.

"Has nothing new been written?" I walk in front of him, dragging my fingertips softly across the spines of the books.

"Mekaia actually wrote all these, he's the first ever fallen angel."

My mouth hangs open, the first one ever? "How old does that make him?"

Rowan shrugs when I look back at him. "Your guess is as good as mine."

He pulls out some books from the shelves and walks towards a table. I think we are the only people in the library, but I'm sure Rowan would say something different. As he lays out the books to the correct pages he would like me to read, I feel a chill go down my spine; someone is watching us. "Rowan," My voice cracks and he turns his head around to look at me. I only see his eyes widen a second before he speeds by me and a crash happens right after. I turn around to see Rowan pinning a man to the ground. Rowan's got a good grip on him, and the man isn't going anywhere but seems to be resisting as much as he can.

"Calm yourself!" The authority in Rowan's voice almost brings me to my knees before the man stops struggling.

"I'm sorry! I didn't know she was spoken for!" Rowan helps the man up, he seems very young. His hair is brown and looks like it's been tossed about and his skin is tan, a mix between Camille and I.

"What the hell were you doing?" I ask him, feeling confident that Rowan has a grip on the back of his shirt, his feet barely on the ground. His green eyes stare into mine before Rowan yanks him to the side,

"Don't look in her eyes."

Woah tough guy, that's not disrespectful to humans. "I wanted to mark you."

I'm sorry, you lost me there. "Mark me?"

Rowan lets out a breath and lets go of his collar. "He's a werewolf looking for his mate. It's like their soulmate." I look pointedly at the boy in front of me, he couldn't be any older than twenty.

"I am definitely not your mate."

He nods and looks back to Rowan, "I'm sorry. Please forgive me."

"Why would you think that she's your mate?"

He shrugs and avoids eye contact with the both of us. "She smells good."

I chuckle slightly and the boy looks back up at me, awe in his eyes. "It's customary for humans to try and smell their best. What's your name?"

He stands and extends his hand, "Marcus, my lady!" I take his hand in mine to shake it and I feel the calluses on them.

"My name is Samara-"

"You can call her Sam." Rowan interrupts me. Now that he's made it a point, I notice that he's the only person who calls me Samara; besides Mekaia and that girl we shall not name.

"That brute over there is Rowan." I guess his name strikes fear into Marcus, because he takes a step away from him.

"Forgive me Rowan, I wasn't aware she was yours."

"I am my own." I state matter-of-factly. Rowan and I may have some connection, but that doesn't mean I am not my own person. I see the hurt in Rowan's eyes but he recovers when he sees me standing tall.

"Samara is my girlfriend."

I guess we are putting a label on it. I blush deeply and add to him, "Rowan is my boyfriend." Marcus seems more relaxed now that we are all, mostly, talking. "Rowan, I'll start reading some of these books if you show Marcus where the werewolf section is? I'm sure he'd like to learn a bit about his history." Rowan gives me an 'are you serious?' look before he motions for Marcus to follow him. Once they are out of sight, I turn back to the table, ready to read all this information and have my head explode with knowledge.

I'm not sure where Rowan and Marcus go, but in their absence I learn quite a bit about the fallen angels. Pretty much everything Rowan told me is in these books, except they're worded like they're from long ago; and they probably are if Mekaia is the one who wrote all these. I find the perfect sacrifice section, that tells all there is to know about it. This is exactly what the killer is doing. Rowan mentioned that he thought it was Mekaia, but I bet after how he acted 'approving me' or whatever, Rowan probably isn't thinking that anymore: which leads us right back to square one. I pull out my phone and type out a couple questions, most of them relate to the possibility of Mekaia being our killer. I don't want to get on Rowan's bad side, but I know that the lives of innocent people need to be put first.

I stand up from the table and gather as many books in my hand as I can. Walking back to the shelf we got them from, I put all of them up except one. I can't reach the top shelf. Before I can go to find Rowan, someone comes behind me, takes the book from my hands and puts it up. I can tell it's him just by the way his body feels against mine. "I got you." His breath hits the inside of my neck and I lean back into him.

"I think we deserve more nights like last night."

Feeling bold in our closeness, I say something risky and hope for a good response. "I think I can arrange that." He starts to kiss my neck and a small moan comes out of my mouth, but that just encourages him. His arms trail down my body and rest on my thighs, pulling me backwards to be flush with his legs. I feel him hardening and I push my hips back against him in a steady rhythm.

"Samara," His voice is dark and I would love nothing more than to continue further with him. As he begins to undo his belt and his pants, I feel the familiar chill of someone watching us.

"Rowan, stop."

He stops undoing his belt and turns me around slowly. "What's wrong? Did I do something?"

"Baby not at all." I cup his face and give him a small kiss. "I just feel a little uncomfortable here. Feels like there's someone watching us."

"I'll go check it out. Stay here, Marcus isn't too far either." I nod and Rowan turns the corner, leaving me in the aisle. I decide to finish cleaning up the books so we can make it home. I walk back out to the table and get the last of the books; however, there's one book that neither of us picked up and it's already opened onto one page.

I run my hands along the page, and the top of the page reads 'Deja Vu.' I don't remember Rowan ever mentioning this. I pick up the book and start reading. My eyes go wide and my breath hitches. Rowan and I are soulmates? No, more importantly than that, I've lived several lifetimes? Is this my last now that I know this? Tears start to leave my eyes and Rowan comes before me in a flash. "Samara? Samara, what's wrong?" I drop the book and it lands flat on the page I was reading. He looks down and his eyes widen just like mine. "Let me explain."

THIRTY TWO

Rowan

Her tears slip over her eyes silently, I want to take away the pain. If only she knew the kind of pain I was feeling too. Pain and rage. Now that she knows about Deja Vu, there's a chance I'll never see her again in my immortal life. There has to be a way out of this. I'll find a way to save her and to save myself from eternal darkness. "You hid this from me?" I'm confused by her question. If we read the same legend, she knows that I couldn't tell her or she may not live another lifetime.

"Samara, I had to. In my five hundred years on this Earth, no one has ever held a flame to you. If I told you about this, you may not live to meet me another time."

"I mean that you're my soulmate."

I chuckle sadly. "That's what you're worried about?" Her face hardens and I realize that laughing was a big mistake.

"This whole situation made me think I was crazy. From almost dying to learning about the supernatural, to feeling this intense connection with you! Sleeping with you for crying out loud." I sit down at the table in front of her and pull her into me. She fights to get away but I won't let her, not after I just got her.

"You want to hear it? Fine. Samara, you are my soulmate. God cast us from Heaven together and the universe has been trying to push us towards each other for five hundred years. I didn't tell you because I just found you. If I told you this, you could die and never come back." She's crying real tears now, her body shaking with every breath she takes. She's so beautiful.

"I *just* found *you*. I've spent five hundred lonely years without you, feeling empty. Meeting you is a breath of fresh air after a fire, or seeing the first ray of sunshine after a hurricane. You scare me and excite me all at once and I am in love with you Samara." Her crying abruptly ends and she stares me down, wiping her tears as she regains her composure. "I am so in love with you it hurts when you're away. To see you cry is poison to my happiness."

"I can't say it right now, Rowan." I try not to let the pang in my chest show on my face when she says it. She can't tell me she loves me after I have proclaimed my love for her to everyone. I risked getting executed for treason for her. I may be immortal, but there are some ways to kill a fallen angel. All of which I would risk for her, and she can't even say she loves me? We both know it to be true.

I think about her for a second, and realize that she has been through too much for me to torment her about something that I know to be true. I know that she loves me, or at least cares about me very deeply. I also trust her with my life, which is something I can say about less than a handful of people. I pull her closer to me, her head going in my neck and I feel her silent tears dampen my shirt. "You don't have to say it. I know." She wraps her arms around me and hugs me as tight as she can.

"I'm sorry."

I shake my head and my hand snakes up her back, pulling her closer. "You do not have to be sorry, Samara." We stand in silence for a couple moments before she pulls away, wiping the remainder of her tears from her face. "You don't have to apologize to me, and I won't apologize to you." I have to make it clear to her that I hurt because she is upset, but that I won't apologize for keeping a secret. Her knowing this information could directly result in her not living anymore lifetimes. "If you didn't find out this information, you would have never known it. Until you're old and you're taking your last breaths on your deathbed, and even then you still wouldn't know it. I would have let you live your whole life without knowing, and God help whoever left that book out, because I will take their immortality away from them and leave them with suffering."

My words take her back. In her sweet, innocent mind, she probably doesn't know that I've killed people. I've fought in wars, killed people for this country and I've killed people for my kind. I would do much worse to someone if they dare mess with her. I rub my thumb over her face, remnants of our time in the aisle flutter through my mind as I imagine my thumb in her mouth, the pad sitting right on her tongue as she moves it side to side. I think she catches onto what I'm thinking and she steps back. "I think it's time we go home." I sigh and nod, quickly realizing that now is not the time, and with the events of today I wonder if there will ever be a time again.

I take her back to her apartment, Camille wakes up as we walk inside and Samara quickly dismisses me. She kisses me quickly and closes the door. I hear her break down on the other side. Instead of breaking down the door and facing off with, yet again, Camille holding a butchers knife, I decide to go back to Mekaia's office and figure out who the fuck messed with Samara.

I burst through the doors to see Mekaia in a meeting with Uriah, "Get out." I don't even look at Uriah, but he jumps up and walks out the door behind me. My eyes are frozen on Mekaia, his turning red by the second; obviously seeing my stare as a challenge. Let him, I'm done correcting myself. I break away from the intense gazes for just a moment to walk over to his bookshelf and point to the empty spot where the Deja Vu book is supposed to be. "Did you show this to Samara?"

His eyes widen and he stands from his desk, his eyes no longer the blood red color. "Rowan, I swear-"

"You told her about the rule! She knows!"

He shakes his head and grabs my shoulders. "Rowan, I did not tell her. That book has always stayed in this office, never once has it left."

I throw his arms off of me. "I beg to differ. It was laid out, already flipped to the page when we were leaving the library. She read all about it." I begin to pace around his office, I worry about Samara. The way she sounded through the door when I left, her sobbing in my arms earlier and knowing that I wasn't there to comfort her right now. Knowing that there may be a time where her presence is no longer on Earth, it sends me into a spiral.

I throw everything off of Mekaia's desk in a fit of rage. My mind blacking out as I throw any and everything I can get my hands on. It all stops when one of my hands lands on Mekaia's face in a punch. The low growl that emits from him snaps my vision back and I put my hands in front of myself to catch him from lunging at me. It doesn't help. In a second he has me pinned up against the wall, holding me by my throat. "Mekaia!" I manage to croak out, he's staring at me with dark red eyes. Maybe this time of me challenging his authority will be my last.

"Listen here Rowan," He lets my throat go just enough for me to breathe, but keeps a steady hold on me. "I didn't give her the book. So I am not your target." I try to look down, showing my respect for him but he keeps my head still, forcing me to look him in the face. "But that doesn't give you the right to disrespect me like you have today. You can either get over it or face my wrath. What is it, huh?" He pushes me farther off the ground, my legs dangling and wanting to plant me back on my own.

"Are you going to join me, and help me find this monster? Or are you going to die right here right now and leave your precious Samara?" Her name snaps me back, anger rushing through me. I use all my strength to push him off me. Mekaia stumbles backwards, a shocked expression plagues his face. He obviously didn't know I was capable.

"One thing we should share with each other, I'm not as weak as you believe me to be. If anything, I'm your equal."

He laughs loudly, "Ha! My equal?" He stalks towards me but stops short, our noses almost touching. "You are nothing but a pipsqueak compared to me." We stand there for a moment in silence, sizing each other up. Both of us know we should fight for the right reasons, him bringing up Samara and me threatening his dominance. However, both of us stand still and breathe for several moments, knowing our smartest decision is to team up and find the real culprit: the one who wants us to fight, the one who wants to kill.

"I will do anything to help you, if you don't challenge me so blatantly again." I nod, accepting his help. Mekaia is the most powerful Fallen Angel, I could use his strength and expertise.

"Whoever killed those people has shown up to Samara's apartment, threatened her, and is blatantly targeting me for investigating this. They have to be stopped."

Mekaia nods and replies, "They will. For now, I need you to be with Samara. If you lose her, there is no hope for us all."

THIRTY THREE

Samara

The hours I've spent crying while Camille holds me are finally taking their toll. I'm exhausted, dehydrated, and hungry. Most of all: I miss Rowan. It's stupid, this soulmate bond thing, it doesn't make any sense to me. I've never had a connection like this with any of my past relationships, and it's foreign to me. It's scary. Now, I know there's a possibility of dying and never experiencing him again. That's the most frightening part- being without him. But I also think about his side; he's immortal, if I die, he will never have me again. I can be happy with him in this lifetime, but I'll always have the thought of him not meeting me ever again.

I decide to write him a letter, in case I don't come back. Maybe he will laugh at me or maybe it'll be the one thing he can hold on to. While I'm at it, I write one for everyone I am close to: Rowan, Camille, Francis, my Mom. By the time I am finished, wet tear stains litter the paper and I worry about them ripping. I fold them neatly and put them in envelopes, stuffing them into the file with my will and important documents.

I hear a stern knock at the door. I'm in my room but I can hear Camille's confusion when she opens the door. "Hey!" My bedroom door flies open, showing a Rowan who seems to be holding it together by a thread. "Hey, get out of here!" Camille comes in after him, her frame almost completely hidden by Rowan.

"No." Rowan is a man of *many* words when he is angry. I have never seen him with true rage before, I think it's better that way. "I will be with you, here."

He points to the spot he's standing and Camille looks around him, staring at me to ask, "Is this okay?" I nod at her and she huffs, giving Rowan one last glance as she walks out of the room, closing the door behind her.

"I want to stay with you." His voice changes. He isn't a demanding man anymore, he's a damaged one, one who sounds like he could break at any moment.

"What if I don't want you to stay?" My question hurts both of us, the thought of not staying together making our hearts crumble. Rowan's eyes leave mine as he looks to the building in front, the one he described watching me on. My mouth gapes open, "You wouldn't even leave me be?"

He shakes his head without hesitation. "You need to be protected."

"I can handle myself."

I blink and he is close enough to kiss me, the wind from his speed hits me and I hold my breath. "I have no doubt of that, Samara. But physically, if someone like me wanted to hurt you," He leans past my face, putting his mouth as close to my ear as he can. "You wouldn't be able to blink before they did."

I shiver and slightly push him away from me. "You can stay." His face breaks into a full grin which quickly fades when I interrupt him, "But no secrets, you are going to be honest to me from here on out. If not, I will kill you."

He gulps, believing me one hundred percent, and nods slowly. He struggles to kick off his shoes, showing that he wants to lay down with me. I move over to allow him room, and he plops down, making the whole mattress move. "I have some questions." He lays on his side to face me, propping his head up with one arm and using his free hand to rub up and down my leg.

"I'll answer you truthfully, as always."

I roll my eyes and take in a deep breath, trying not to focus on the way his hand feels slowly creeping up my leg. "When we slept together, did you know about us being soulmates?" He doesn't stop what he's doing but he slowly nods his head.

"I had found out the day before."

Even though I don't regret it, guilt floods me for some reason. I hate the idea of him keeping that secret from me. "I didn't sleep with you because you were my soulmate. I slept with you because I'm in love with you. I think I have been since we first actually met." I don't say anything, but my heart wants to say the words my head is too scared to.

"You said you only just found me, how do you know this isn't my first lifetime?" Saying the question sounds insane and I barely get it out without stuttering. This seems like a movie, not my real life. This can't be my life.

"I honestly don't know. You were cast down to be a human doppelganger. You could've lived as many lives in my five hundred years, but this is the first one I've found you in."

Rowan says it nonchalantly, but I know it's deeper than that. He's just been feeling empty, with no one by his side, for five hundred years. I lean down and cup his face. "I am here now. Don't let me go anywhere."

A devilish grin comes on his face as he leans closer to me. "There's not a place in the world you could hide from me now." If he wasn't my boyfriend, soulmate-thing, I would've been scared. But it's comforting knowing someone cares about me like this where I know they will always find me.

"Who do you think it is?" Rowan asks me, taking me by surprise as he lays back down on the bed.

I take in a breath, knowing that my answer will probably hurt him, "Mekaia."

He moves his head back slightly. "Why Mekaia?"

"Come on, Mekaia is the oldest fallen angel. He's been away from Heaven longer than anyone and he's starting to lose his mind. Blood red eyes that I saw at my door are just a coincidence to Mekaia's eyes that change when he's mad?" I guess my point has finally registered by the way he stays still, processing the information.

"No, it's not him. He's the one who sent me here to be with you, so I can watch over you." Did he only come because Mekaia said?

"You said that you wanted to stay with me, but was it really because Mekaia sent you?" He can tell how it sounds and he can tell that he messed up. I move slightly away from him, distancing myself from the repeated disappointment of the lies he spews.

"No, he told me I could come to you, to protect you and be here with you. I didn't do it because he said, I did it because I wanted to."

"But what if he told you to stay away from me? Would you follow what he says?"

He sits straight up and moves closer to me, closing the distance that I separated. "Why would you even think about asking me that?"

He leans in to try and hug me but I put my hand on his chest to stop him. "Answer the question." He huffs and holds my hand closer to his chest.

"Samara, do you feel that?" I focus on the pressure under my hand, his pulse. "The only reason this beats, the only reason I am here, is because of you." He brings my other hand up to cup his face and he leans into it, breathing against my skin. "You are half of my soul. I would do the impossible for you. Damn Heaven or Hell."

He may stumble over his words all the time and get himself into predicaments, but he sure knows how to get out of them. He puts his hand behind my head and pulls me closer to kiss him. Slow and methodical, tender and caring. I'm happy we found each other. "So wait," I pull back and look at him. "If you don't think it's Mekaia, then who is it?" He shrugs and sits up to look at me better. "I don't know. It's a fallen angel for sure, but there's thousands if not millions of us. It could be anyone."

"Instead of figuring out who it is, why don't we figure out their next victim?"

Rowan signs in defeat, "We could spend all night listing off every organ that they've taken in their kills, but it won't make a difference because we don't know what they've gotten from the black market." He's right. We have no idea how long this has been going on or how many organs they've collected. This situation is not on our side, and I'm not sure if we will be able to figure this out.

"I don't want more innocent people dying." Rowan agrees with me by pulling me closer and kissing the top of my head.

"We will figure it out." Rubbing my hands up and down his back, I feel his muscles as he breathes. The way his breath slows, showing that he's almost asleep.

"You're perfect." He smiles and I chuckle slightly, until I sit straight up as gasp.

"Samara?" Rowan jumps up beside me, scanning the room, probably thinking we are in imminent danger. "What's wrong?"

I stare at him wide eyed, "You're perfect."

He rolls his eyes, "Thank you for the compliment but I was trying to sleep."

"No! Rowan, you *are* perfect."

He shrugs, "I am not following this at all." I stand up from the bed and grab his hand, leading him to the bathroom. Facing him in front of the mirror, I stand beside him and allow him to take his appearance in. His blue eyes, high cheekbones, tan skin, fit body. "Oh my god." He gets it!

"If there's one thing we know, the last kill, the body, will be a fellow Fallen Angel.

THIRTY FOUR

Rowan

The thought of a fallen angel killing another makes my skin crawl, my blood boil. It's unheard of to kill your own kind, but I guess a psychotic murderer doesn't fit between the spectrum. I stare at myself in the mirror and see Samara standing beside me. If anyone is perfect, she is. "I don't understand how we are perfect though?" She puts her hand on my stomach, lighting a fire in my gut.

"You don't have to see it, cause everyone else does." She pushes me slightly back, making enough room for her to slide and sit on the vanity, her legs around my waist. "You, Uriah, Mekaia, even Rose, are all beautiful people. Like, unnecessarily beautiful people."

Slight jealousy fumes through my brain, and the way she looks right now, hair tousled, pajamas on and her eyes looking up at me; it was enough to light that flame from earlier. Taking a step forward to eliminate any space between us, she has to look almost straight up to make eye contact with me. I put one of my hands on her face, cupping it as she leans in closer, the other on her hip, laying flat so I can keep her in place. I lean down slowly, keeping my eyes on her and I don't make my move until I see that she's closed her eyes.

I don't kiss her fast or sloppy, just hard. Holding her face close to mine, it's tough to breathe but all worth the loss of oxygen. Her hands go to my shirt and tug, I break away for just a moment to help her lift my shirt over my head before I go back to her lips. Except she stops me and pushes my leg down, bringing me to a knee in front of her. She's higher than me now, knowing that it puts her in a position of power. "What do you want?"

The leg that pushed me down now pulls me forward to the drawstrings on her shorts. "I want what you did last time."

Her voice drips with seduction and nervousness, her normal combination but in this situation: me below her and her with all the power, it's irresistible. I grab the skin of her thigh in my mouth and begin leaving hickeys up them. No one should be able to see her thighs this high besides me, it's a win-win. Her breathy moans fill my ear and I reach up to palm her breasts through her shirt, feeling her nipples get hard instantly. Her back arches and pushes her closer to me and closer to the edge of the vanity.

I try to stand up, but her leg is still draped over my back. Instead, I drag her shorts down as far as they can go, no doubt they'll be stretched by the way they rest behind my head. I blow gently on her center, driving her insane just like the first time we did this.

Dragging my tongue slowly upwards, I taste all of her sweetness that pools for me. Her moans fill the bathroom and add to the thick heat of tension that we feel. Our bodies buzz where we aren't touching, needing to be closer. Her moans become quicker, shallower, and I know she's almost done. Stroking my tongue up and down, I quicken the pace and press a finger inside her, tilting up. She takes one sharp breath and holds it before she exhales and fills the air with loud, throaty moans. I continue to play with her throughout her orgasm, and once her legs go limp around my shoulders, I shimmy upwards and undo my belt buckle.

Her shorts fall off when I stand, but her legs stay wrapped around me, not sure but not against whatever is going to happen next. I let my pants and boxers fall to my ankles, revealing a fully nude version of myself to her. Her hands trail invisible lines from around my neck down my torso and up my back, just to repeat once again. Her eyelids flutter as she looks up at me. She stops tracing my body and takes off her shirt, her beautiful body exposed to me completely and fully. I step as close as I can to her, the cold vanity radiating around us, drawing us closer to each other for warmth.

The closer I move to her, and the more warmth I feel being emitted from her, the larger I grow. Her skin erupts into goosebumps as we make contact, my tip slides up her wet center, and once again I am at her mercy. My skin lights a fire in her as she adjusts her body, ready to take me right here on the vanity.

How did we get to this? I wonder to myself, but then I remember, she's too much of a spitfire to not get what she wants. Her hand reaches down and grabs me, aligning me with her entrance, as her legs come up behind me, ready for another orgasm and pull me into her slowly. With a little bit of guidance, it doesn't take me long until I am in her, filled to the brim. She draws a long breath out of me when she moves her hips first, it comes out more like a hiss.

Control is something I am an expert at, and this woman tests my resolve every time she is near me. The back and forward motion of her hips, the quick breaths and small moans that come from her mouth, the way her hair falls over her shoulder and almost covers her breasts, all of it is enough to make me want to rip into her and never let go. The heat from our bodies begins to fog up the mirror and creates a damp sheet covering the vanity, causing Samara to slightly lose her position. Before she completely slides off the vanity, I pick her up, and carry her back to the bed.

Fear and excitement cloud her eyes as my hands rest on her ass, my face full of mischief. I think I may have one up on her, that is until she swings her weight around and ends up on top of me. Pushing me down with her arms, she repeats the steps from the bathroom: putting me into place, slowly sliding down, and the breathy moan that comes out of her makes me know that this feels deeper for her.

She starts to bounce slowly, but I stop her and grab her hips, taking the lead. Pushing her away and pulling her back towards me, I help her understand the way this feels, the better way to be on top. It doesn't take her long to understand, because the next thing I know she is pushing me back down with her hands on my chest. Her eyes close and she leans her head back, I get a full view of the front of her body and know that God's creation is truly perfect.

There's no way he didn't create her and not spend a million years crafting her beauty from stone.

Once again, her pace quickens and I can't do anything but watch her, feel her. The fire in my groin is growing, but it will definitely outlast Samara. She sputters around me, her movements too quick for her own good as she holds her breath and then moans loudly while still moving. Her body falls onto my chest, me still inside her, and I rub her head and then trail my hands up and down her back. Her voice is small and timid when she speaks, like she's scared to be too loud even after all she's been through. "I love you."

My throat tightens and I can hear her heartbeat, strong and true. She means it. I pull her closer to me and flip us over, the fire in my body is more than I can take. "Samara, I love you." Her small smile begins to fade as my control snaps and I begin to thrust into her. I hold her legs against my torso, they come up and meet around my neck, holding me in place as I pull out and thrust into her. My arms have her legs locked to my torso, she's not going anywhere.

Her voice flutters throughout the room, "*Rowan.*" The actions of her saying my name, the way she's tightening around me and her moans fluttering out of her make me feel like my skin is on fire. Everytime we are near, a second without her touch feels like death. A second with her touch lights a fire that can only be satisfied with her: her voice, her touch, her love.

I don't want this to end, her swallowing me inside her, taking me so well, I'd be happy here forever.

The pit in my stomach is rising and I know I won't last much longer with the way she's pushing down to meet every thrust. I untie her legs from around my neck and flush my body against hers, the new angle making me grunt in satisfaction.

Reaching down between her legs, I put the pad of my thumb on her sensitive bud, making her hips rise off the bed and come closer. "*Samara,*" Her name leaves my mouth but I can barely hear it, I could've not even said it at all, but the way she's looking at me, I know that she heard me. "I love you. Fuck, I love you so much," My thrusts become sloppy and relentless, any second now and it'll be game over.

"Rowan," God her voice. "I love-" I push our lips together as we come undone, our moans fluttering through our connected mouths. I can feel myself rubbing against her walls and I can feel her tightening and releasing me. Sloppy and feverish is the best way to describe us in this moment, just so overcome with sensual satisfaction that there's not much else to do but sit and breathe afterwards.

My brain is filled with the love that I have for her. Samara is my destiny, she is the moon that moves the tides, the rain that feeds the Earth, the sun that makes me grow. The only thing that holds a candle to my love for her, is my fear of losing her, which is growing more possible by the day.

THIRTY FIVE

Samara

For the past week, all we have been doing is sleeping, eating, and having sex. Ever since I told him I love him, we've been doing it a lot more than normal. Our soulmate bond continues to grow stronger, and sometimes it's a lot for me to handle. Knowing how much I love him, the thought of losing him, the thought of me dying: it's too much. But everytime I think about giving up and letting it all go, Rowan's there to remind me to never give up.

The past week we've been together, nothing has popped up on the radar that worries us. It's eerily quiet, the kind of quiet that makes you feel like everything is going to break loose. Mekaia has called in extra security during this time, now that Rowan told him the last piece of the puzzle is to kill a fallen angel, everyone is on edge.

Rowan will barely let me out of his sight and I'm rarely at work. Francis has called to check on me a couple times, but I just keep telling her I have an unstoppable stomach bug. I've managed to write more of my article, but I've accepted there's no point. Whether I stay at Shapiro Informatics or not, the truth can never come out about the true killer.

I've tried not to think about what happens if I lose my job. Maybe Rowan could help me find something? Maybe I could be one of his human contacts now? That would be favorable, doing something more important. He would never go for it, he would just ramble on about how I'd be in too much danger. Camille has been enjoying this extra time with Rowan and I, she's even brought Jamie over for dinner a couple nights. I can't say that Rowan and I haven't walked in on Camille and Jamie kissing, but for her sake I pretend I haven't seen anything, even with the rosy blush forming on their cheeks.

"I haven't heard from Mekaia today, I think I might go check on him." Rowan removes the covers from the bed and walks to the dresser in my room. Let's just say that he's moved some clothes in. I watch him get dressed but don't say anything, instead I just sit there and take in his beauty. The way his muscles move and the way his hair slightly flows with every turn. "What?"

His voice draws me back and I shake my head at his question. "Nothing,"

"You were staring at me and practically drooling." I scoff and pull the covers up farther so they're sitting around my neck, hiding my bare body underneath.

"You wish." He walks to the end of the bed and begins to crawl up it on his hands and knees. His bicep muscles bulge as he stalks up the bed, getting closer and closer as a smirk becomes plastered on his face.

"Come on, Samara. You can tell me." His hands find my waist through the sheets which are feeling incredibly thin right now. Fluttering fingertips grasp at my sides as they move up painfully slow to my chest. He traps me below him, his leg pressed between mine and his hands caging me under him. I smell his shampoo from his slightly damp hair, the way the woodsy scent wafts around us. It makes me feel like we aren't in this concrete jungle, like I'm back home.

"I just told you, I wasn't and you're imagining things." His head dips down to my neck, blowing air softly on it before his lips come down and slowly kiss up to my jawline. His teeth nip at my jaw and he stays close to my ear, not ignoring the way my body presses me further into his leg for some pressure.

"I think you're lying."

I shake my head slightly, "I'd never lie to you." I mean it, sincerely, and he can tell this by the way he holds himself up over me, staring down into my eyes.

"I know." He doesn't say anything else but is silently proclaiming his love, this soulmate bond has started allowing us to feel each others' emotions. It's not foolproof but it gives us a slight indication, which is enough for Rowan to use it to his best, and worst, ability. We haven't learned too much more about this bond, and Mekaia has been reluctant to tell us anything. Part of me thinks he knows exactly what this bond is capable of and he's scared of it. No matter what Rowan thinks, I don't trust Mekaia as blindly as he does.

"Be safe?" I ask him as he gets up from his camp on top of me.

"I always am, I'm just going to see Mekaia." A slight breath leaves my body and I'm trying my best not to feel worried or agitated. It seems like a worthless effort when Rowan looks at me and shakes his head. "What? You still don't trust him?" I slowly stand from the bed, making my way to the bathroom to put on my robe, but also trying to avoid this conversation.

"I didn't say that."

"But you thought about it." No point in avoiding something that was bound to happen from the start. I tie my robe around my waist and cover myself, crossing my arms across my chest.

"Are we really going to ignore the fact that all the signs point to Mekaia?" I lean against the threshold in the bathroom and stare up at him, he's agitated and it continues to grow as he runs his hands through his hair.

"Mekaia has been nothing but honest to us. He has no reason to lie or do anything of this sort."

I take slow steps towards him and count on my fingers as I talk, "He's been away from heaven the longest, he's the first fallen, he knows all the history, his eyes turn red, you can't find him half the time."

Rowan shakes his head like he's trying to keep my voice out. "Look, I get it. Your dad died and you haven't had a Father figure in a long time," *Rage*. "But Mekaia is the only Father I have ever known and he wouldn't do anything to hurt me. He blessed our relationship-"

"Blessed our relationship?" He might not know he messed up with the Father comment, but now he knows he's in trouble.

"Don't you ever say anything about my father or how he is not here ever again. I have grieved for years and I don't need to have all of that healing ripped up by you thinking I don't like Mekaia because my dad died." Venom drips from my voice and if looks could kill, Rowan and I would be in an eternal fight right now. "Mekaia might not do anything to hurt you, but what about everyone else? You're telling me in the five hundred years that you have been here on Earth, Mekaia has not done one single thing to raise your doubts?" He sits quietly for a moment, and I know he's found the action that causes his doubts. "That's what I thought."

I walk out of the room without giving him a second glance, and I feel his regret come off in waves. He shuffles behind me and walks out, following behind me. Camille sits up on the couch and raises her eyes at me, I shake my head, silently telling her that we don't need to talk about it. "Samara,"

"Don't." My one word is a sentence enough when I walk over to the door and open it, signaling him to get out. "Go see Mekaia, like you planned."

He shakes his head and stands his ground, "We need to talk, I didn't mean it like that."

I shrug and motion a hand to the door once again. "Doesn't matter how you meant it. Go see Mekaia." He steps closer and I take a step back. "I am telling you politely to go complete your plans. Do not make me tell you to get out of our home." His eyes soften when I call it 'our home,' but frankly right now I just want him out.

Camille makes a move to get off the couch and make her way to the kitchen, Rowan passes her and walks to the door, gives me a kiss on my forehead and says, "I'll be back later." I close the door with a slam and stare at it for a blank moment, the white paint stares back at me with no remorse. He shouldn't have said that. We shouldn't have had that conversation.

"Well, that was tense." Camille, the moderator, breaks the uneven silence in the apartment. I turn to face her and see her holding a knife, maybe the same one she threatened him with before. She sees my obvious look against it and shrugs, "Look if he turns on you, I've got to keep you safe." I think about this for a moment, would Rowan really turn on me? No. Even if this soulmate bond wasn't real, he wouldn't do that, he would still do the right thing and that is not hurting Camille or myself. "What happened?" Camille's voice brings me back to attention and I walk over to the counter to take a seat.

"It started with Mekaia."

"I haven't met him but I don't like him. Seems like a prick."

I shake my head at her, "He's not too bad, but obviously we feel a little different than Rowan does." Camille is doing her own thing, fixing herself something to eat and she makes me a glass of water.

"What does that mean?"

I take a sip before I speak again, the anger sitting just below the surface. "It means, he thinks of Mekaia like a Father, and he thinks the reason I don't like Mekaia is because I don't have one." This frustrates me. I do have a father, just because he is no longer in this world doesn't mean I have always been without him. He is still with me in small ways, like how the freckle on my cheekbone is from him, the color of my hair, the way the accent may come out when I'm angry.

"Look, not all of us have an opportunity to know our real father, or even have good ones."

Oh no, she's lecturing. "Rowan is doing what he knows, defending Mekaia. He's been doing that for five hundred years. How would you feel if someone was accusing your dad of being a murderer?" I understand what she's saying, but I have this feeling that our bad guy is Mekaia.

"All of the signs point to-"

"It doesn't matter what they point to." She interrupts me before I can even finish. By now, she is standing in front of me on the opposite side of the counter. "Lawfully and logically, yes, maybe Mekaia is our bad guy who is a killer. But emotionally? This is Rowan's oldest friend that we are talking about. He will defend him until he can't anymore, then he will have to worry about what to do and feel afterwards."

Camille never ceases in her surprises, I've always known that she was mature for her age, but she's taking our recent situation in stride. I understand that I may have overreacted, but as a man who is supposed to be my soulmate, he should have more common sense than to talk about anyone's deceased father. "He shouldn't have said that about your dad. But, you need to look at it from his point of view." I nod slowly, agreeing with her. There isn't much I can do at this point but cool off and give it a little time before Rowan comes home. He's probably going to be busy with finding more leads, considering there's been nothing this week.

"My emotions are running high and this case isn't helping anything."

She walks from the kitchen and goes back to sitting on the couch. "Obviously this soulmate bond is taking its toll."

I nod. I am so worn out from this past week, physically and emotionally. "We keep finding new things out about the bond. Now we can feel each other's emotions."

"You are literally in an episode from The Twilight Zone." I chuckle at her response. The clouds outside make it appear darker and the raindrops liter the windows of the apartment. I sigh and make my way to sit beside her.

"Camille?"

"Yeah, Sam?" I grab her hand and hold it, I don't miss the way she turns to look at me. Her chocolate skin shines in the lights and her brown eyes twinkle, but with worry.

"I love you."

"Don't you dare get sappy on me." We both laugh and she doesn't say it back, but I know she means it. What she doesn't know is that I've got the papers written up to legally adopt her. I'm waiting for the right moment to tell her, and the moment after Rowan and I have an argument doesn't seem to be the best. I want her to know this home will be stable, healthy, and happy while she is in it, so she doesn't have to worry about anything like last time.

"Sam, do you know what we can do to help Rowan?" This takes me back, Camille always thinks that Rowan can handle himself, and it touches me that she wants to help him.

"What can we do?" She stands and looks down at me before she grabs my hands and pulls me up from the couch.

"We can find out who the real killer is."

THIRTY SIX

Rowan

How dare she think I meant it like that? I would never disrespect her or her father and what was left of their relationship. I could feel how conflicted she was, and now it's only getting worse being away from her. Her emotions are all over the place and it's making staying focused more difficult than I intended. A week straight with her to then being kicked out is taking its toll, I want nothing more than to be with her, wrapped up in the sheets with not a care in the world. Finding Mekaia and finding out who this real killer is needs to be a number one priority; but my brain will not allow me to forget the sounds of Samara.

Arriving at Mekaia's office, it looks like a tornado has gone through. Books and papers are ripped to shreds and cover the floor, while glass shards litter the ground from pictures and artifacts. The desk where

Rose sits has blood stains on it, the only way a fallen angel can bleed is if they're in a fight with a fellow angel. I begin to worry: is my time up to find out who the killer is? Have they taken Rose? Where is Mekaia?

"Mekaia! Rose! Uriah?" My screams are desperate and my heart begins to race. Are they in danger?

"Rowan…" My head snaps to Rose's desk and I walk behind it to be faced with her body slumped on the floor, blood pooling out of her side. Her face paler than usual, her lips chapped and her breathing ragged.

"Rose!" I lift her head up to sit in my lap. She coughs and blood begins to leak out her mouth. "Rose!" My voice cracks and I realize I'm on the verge of losing it.

"What happened? Where are the others?" I am looking down at her and realizing that I could be the last thing she sees before she dies, before her breaths stop coming and her eyes shut forever.

"They took them," I pick her up bridal style, and her breathing becomes more shallow, she groans as I stand. "Stop,"

"No, Rose." I shake my head and spread my wings as we leave this place, "I have to get you to the nearest hospital. They'll take care of you." Modern medicine could work on a fallen angel as long as no supernatural injuries occured like a poisoned weapon or a slice of our wings.

The droplets of rain fall through the clouds and feel like needles pricking my skin. Fly faster, fly harder, get her to safety. My brain races with the thought of what is going on with Mekaia and Uriah. Who really did this? Who hurt Rose and took them? I take Rose to the back entrance of the closest hospital, the police department isn't the only place we have connections. A fellow fallen is waiting beside the door, urging others to get a stretcher. "Rowan," The nurse looks up to me and it shouldn't surprise me that she knows my name, but it does. Rose, Uriah and I are all well known in our world simply because we are so close to Mekaia.

I can say I'm a prick though, before I met Samara, it wouldn't have bothered me to know that I have no clue who she is but she knows me. I wouldn't have thought anything different. "What happened to her?" Her question brings me back out of my daze as I set Rose down on the stretcher.

"I don't know. I found her like this." She rips open the bottom of Rose's shirt to reveal a deep cut that's bleeding out faster each minute. She's fading.

"We will take care of her." They begin to walk through the doors and I grab the girl's hand. She's younger than I am, it looks like she's pretty calm in this situation.

"Put the word out that Mekaia is missing. So is Uriah." When I reveal this information, her demeanor slips just a little, but she quickly covers it up once more.

"I'll spread the word."

Getting the word out that Mekaia has been taken should raise the alarm just enough to help find him quickly. The slight clouds that litter the sky have turned into black storm clouds, ready to drop at any moment. The wind shifts and the once comfortable air turns cold. The tension between me and the world hangs in the air, the balance threatening to tip. Whatever has been happening these past couple weeks, or months, it's coming to crest now. Right now.

In the blink of an eye, rain is plowing the concrete jungle below the uneasy sky. Rose is taken care of, she's safe. Before I go and locate Mekaia and Uriah, I have to get to Samara and get her safe. The killer seems to have an interest in Samara, from showing up to her apartment to watching her through her windows. Although, I doubt their interest in Samara is as much as their interest in me.

Samara came to the conclusion that a fallen angel would be the final kill for a perfect sacrifice. Mekaia and Uriah aren't the best options for that, neither is Rose, which is probably why they tried killing her. If anyone in the inner circle is most fit for the sacrifice, it's me. A loyal soldier who follows the orders he's given, even though I've broken a few rules lately. Rose was a distraction to get further away with Mekaia and Uriah, they seem to be serving as bait.

Whoever this killer is, they know I'll come after them. They also know that I will protect the people I care about before anything. That starts with making sure Samara and Camille are okay. Flying through the rain, using the darkness from the clouds as a cover, I race to Samara's apartment. It hasn't been long since I left, but there's always a possibility that she went to work or took Camille somewhere.

Right now, she needs to be there, with me. When I get to the door, it's locked but I don't hear anyone inside. If she was still mad at me, she wouldn't be trying to keep quiet. One swift shoulder to the door and the lock has snapped and I am inside. Everything is as when I left, neat and tidy, besides Camille's desk in the living room. Samara's perfume fills my nose, but it's only remnants of it, fading into the distance.

I pull my phone from my pocket, surprised that it's working considering it's like a hurricane outside. No doubt people are going to pay attention to the weather changing like this-like magic. I dial Samara and get no answer; of course, she's still upset with me. I dial Camille next, she finally answers. "Samara would like her apology in chocolates and a bottle of wine." Any other time this conversation may have gone a different way, and maybe I would have gone right to the store to get her these items.

"Well I guess she's just going to have to let me save her life and hope that makes it up." I hear Samara's voice over the phone, her confusion evident when I hear Camille turn to her. "Where are you guys?"

"Why should we-"

"Samara." I cut her off and she stopped interjecting. "Whatever these murders have been building up to, it's happening. Where. Are. You." It's not a question anymore, it's a command.

I have to find her. No one knows how the perfect sacrifice works, or what happens after. With the attitude and the viciousness of the murderer, I doubt it will be good. "We went back to the bar where we met Jeckel."

"You took Camille to a bar?" I hear her huff over the phone, maybe trying to be a parent isn't the best idea right now.

"Don't you lecture me. It was her idea. We were trying to get ahead of the game."

"I'm coming to you." I don't give them any time to reply before I am out the door, shutting it with no purpose, and making my way there. It was never far from her home to begin with, but the next couple of minutes feels like the years it took me to become accustomed to this world. Seeing her raven hair sway in the wind, being made damp by the rain, the cinder blocks on my shoulders break immediately. I savor the warmth of her embrace, remembering the curves of her body and the classic smell of her perfume. Everything moves in slow motion, her blinking, her breathing, the way the world stops around us.

Except, it actually stops moving.

THIRTY SEVEN

Samara

Once Rowan's arms leave from around me, his scent dissipating, the warmth leaving me, I feel something heavy on my chest. Camille and I share a glance, feeling the same way. "What is that?" Rowan's concerned voice comes in before either of us can answer the empty question. "What is it? What's wrong?"

I shake my head as his hands hold my arms, keeping me in place. "I'm not sure, it feels harder to breathe, like the air's thicker." His worry is hidden behind a confident facade, I know better. If it's dealing with me, he's definitely losing it a bit.

"It's the opposite for me, a weight is completely off my shoulders."

"Look!" Camille's voice draws us back to the inside of the once lively bar that is now frozen in time. Everyone is still, not breathing, not blinking. Except for Camille, Rowan and I, standing in the entryway with confused looks on our faces. The clock hands aren't moving and even though the wind is blowing on Rowan, Camille and I, everyone else is completely still.

"Rowan?"

The worry in my voice is evident, his facade starts to slip. Tingles run up my back and Rowan glances behind me and his eyes widen. "I think this only affects humans." Camille shakes her head as she turns around and sees other people walking away from us, wings splitting from their backs.

"But, we are human?" I grab Camille's hand, trying to comfort her in ways I'm not sure work right now.

"But both of you have touched a fallen angel before." It's true. Obviously Rowan and I have touched and he's carried Camille out of her father's house.

"So it only affects humans who are completely separated from the supernatural world?" Rowan nods, confirming Camille's hypothesis.

"What does that mean for us?"

"It means whoever is plotting this, needs all of us for something." I'll be damned if they hurt either one of them, I'll protect them with my life. But, with me just being human, it may just be in vain. Rowan grabs both of our hands and begins leading us to the outside of the alley where the heavy street traffic is.

Hoping it was all a trick, we turn onto the street and hope for the best, just for it to come crashing down. Everyone is frozen: walkers, runners, cyclists, traffic, billboards. Nothing is moving from the spot it was in when it became hard to breathe. "Rowan, what do we do?" He's looking around frantically, trying to figure out the best course of action. Figures with black wings fly by us fast enough for Camille and me to lose our balance. Rowan grabs Camille by her arm and loops his free arm around my waist, drawing me in closer.

"Whatever this is, it's happening fast."

The thunder begins to roar through the sky and lightning strikes somewhere close. Camille covers her ears and I blend into Rowan. "Look, Samara," Rowan pushes me away but keeps hold of me with one hand on my waist. He reaches for Camille's arm and brings her towards us, in a huddle. "Mekaia and Uriah are missing." If my heart hadn't dropped before, it is vanishing at this point. Did Mekaia finally take Uriah for the sacrifice? Why would he leave Rowan and I alone? "Rose is injured, she can't remember who took them."

This is serious, and I think Camille feels my worry radiating off of me. "What are we supposed to do?" I look between Camille and Rowan, his face blank with no ideas.

"What if we just go back to my apartment and wait this out?" Rowan shakes his head, quickly dismissing it.

"Absolutely not. This killer knows where you live, it's not safe for you there and I can't protect you. I have to go find Mekaia and Uriah." I know those words shouldn't hurt as much as they do, but I try my best to hide the look on my face when he cups my cheek in his hand. "I'm going to take you to my apartment. I've been at your place long enough and I'm confident that it's not Mekaia. He won't hurt you." I also try to hide my disbelief, and if he sees it he doesn't say anything in retaliation.

Rowan spreads his wings from his shirt, the rain starting to pick up now. "It's not going to feel good but this is the fastest way to get to my apartment." He holds Camille to his left and me to his right, tight and surely, with no doubt in his mind about dropping us. I trust him, we've done this before, and during that time I was screaming, thrashing and passing out to dead weight, so this seems a lot easier. Although to Camille, it makes her uneasy, which is to be expected. "I got you. Trust me, Camille." Rowan pleads with her softly as her fear slowly dies down, she nods slowly and grips Rowan like we'll slip through his fingers.

It's not as much trouble as I originally thought to carry us, and we're at his apartment in no time, drenched and out of breath. My body is numb from the coldness of the remnant water, a feeling of pins and needles crawls throughout my skin from the intensity of the rain. "Both of you need to dry off and stay warm, I don't need either of you getting sick."

"Yes Dad." Camille responds without missing a beat as he lays us both a change of clothes on the bed.

"Since time has stopped," He continues without batting an eye at Camille's comment. "Seems like whatever is about to go down, the Heaven's never wanted humans to see it." As he finishes his sentence, thunder and lightning shake the house and rattle our senses. A white streak of light illuminates the whole city above central park, which we have a decent view of from Rowan's apartment.

"What is that?" The light dims but is still apparent as figures begin to descend from the sky. Figures with white wings. "Oh my god." Rowan and I say at the same time.

"Is that-"

"Heavenly angels." Rowan finishes Camille's question and we all exchange looks. Rowan was right, whatever this perfect sacrifice is, it's happening right now, and we are in the middle of it. "I have to go." Rowan is the first to speak after our realization.

"I'm sorry, what? You're going towards the fight?" He nods, changing his jacket and running his hands through his hair.

"I have to."

"To what? Save Mekaia? Save Uriah? They are just as strong as you, they can handle themselves."

Camille is shocked at the words coming out of my mouth. I have always been an advocate for helping people whenever you can. They were kidnapped, it's obvious. It's also pretty obvious that they were more than likely injured during that time. "Samara, I am not going to do this with you." I scoff and shake my head, motioning for Camille to give us a second. She slowly makes her way to the bathroom, even though I know she can hear everything through that door like a piece of paper.

"You have probably spent your five hundred years on this Earth, and God only knows how long in Heaven, cleaning up other people's messes." He shakes his head and walks up to me.

"Have you ever thought that you don't want me throwing myself into the fire because you are afraid I'm going to get burned?" I think about his question, and he's right. I love him unconditionally and I'm worried about him not coming back to me. "I have always been the person to rush into things head first, to protect the people I care about. I've fought wars for Mekaia, I've helped him when he's hurt, I've killed for him." His words take me back, and I have to start accepting that Rowan hasn't always been the good guy. He might not even be a good guy now, but just someone who wants to keep the balance from tipping one way or the other. He would do all this for Mekaia.

Does he care about anyone else that way? Does he care about me that way? "Samara, I can feel the jealousy washing over you. It's not like that." Suddenly I'm filled with embarrassment, and I know he can feel that too by the way he chuckles softly. He brings his hands up to cup my face. "Do not compare the way I feel about Mekaia or Uriah, or even Rose, to the way I feel about you." My heart would normally swell up out of my chest, but under the circumstances of an inevitable battle, the words make me worry that this is goodbye.

"You are my soulmate. You are the oxygen that fills my lungs, the rain that dances on my face, the sun that dries my tears. You are the early morning sounds of birds and the late night sound of crickets before my slumber." Silent tears begin to fall from my eyes at his declaration. Now might be the absolute worst time for this, but I really want to be *with him* right now. "You are the other half of me, the simple reason that I am alive and on this Earth today. My whole purpose is to serve, love, and protect you. Whatever you say, it shall be done."

I want to tell him to not go, that I want him to stay with Camille and I and leave this place. Let's go have a house in the countryside, with a house big enough for Camille to have Jamie over and then her own artroom, for us to have a skylight in our room and make love under the stars, to fly to the top of the hillside and watch the sunrise. I want to tell him that I love him, and that for the rest of my mortal life, I am his.

But I don't.

I don't tell him any of this, my emotions conflict as he waits for my response. Nothing I can say would make this better, the gloomy feeling of a goodbye hanging over us like the clouds outside. "Samara."

Rowan's voice draws me back to full attention in front of him. "I have to go."

Hot tears prick my eyes and my throat tenses up, I have to keep it together. He mutters to me, softly but surely. "I love you, more than anything the entire universe has to offer me. I'd pick you each time."

I smile sadly as silent tears fall once more, "I love you. Come back to me." I say it as an order and not as a question. The only way this ends is him coming back to me.

"Samara, my love, I would burn down the whole world just to come back to you."

THIRTY EIGHT

Rowan

My chest pains me as I leave the apartment, Samara, and Camille behind. My words ring in my ears, showing me the result of the promise I gave her.

I would burn down the whole world just to come back to you.

They should be safe in my apartment. The battle seems like it's going to happen in Central Park, a good spot away from people, people that are moveable and are not going to remember a single thing about today after it's over. The only people who will remember are the supernatural and humans touched by the supernatural. Samara and Camille will live in secrecy of the true world and what happened today.

The Earth feels like it's shaking, like it's being ripped apart from all sides with the descent of the heavenly angels. Even though clouds line the sky, the one hole in the sky is so bright the whole filter of the world shifts. I can barely make out the battle line of fallen angels versus heavenly angels. They have us outnumbered completely, but fallen angels fight dirty. I don't expect this to be any different.

Mekaia and Uriah are sitting on a makeshift altar, both of them are black and blue and chained down. I can tell they are exhausted from blood loss considering they're shirtless and fresh scars line their body. The altar is a circle that surrounds them, but the scariest part is that the different organs that have gone missing from the murders, are also splayed out on the altar, surrounding my two best friends.

Samara was right, this is the perfect sacrifice, it's happening. But who is the culprit? Who is the sick person doing this?

Before I can move forward to help them, an energy wall is put up, no doubt by the heavenly angels. Their perfect sacrifice is coming to a start, and they want to check things out. "Sinners before me, say your names." I hate them, I hate the way their voices chase away the cold and engulf me in a field of warmth. Similar to how Samara makes me feel, except she accepts me for who I am, she accepts my love. *They* kicked me out for loving her.

"Uriah."

"Mekaia."

The heavenly angel is a man, with blonde hair and blue eyes. His high cheekbones don't hide the fear and shock in his face as they finish talking. My head turns to the side as I watch the conversation unfold.

"Mekaia?" His voice is barely a whisper. I'm not sure if it's because of the bloodloss, trauma, or just disbelief, but Mekaia turns his head upwards and recognizes the man before him.

"Deklan?" His voice was barely audible.

Mekaia tries to move and get closer to him, but the man, Deklan, holds up his hand, signaling for him to stop. "Do not come any closer, offering."

Those words break Mekaia as he slumps back down beside Uriah. "Fallen angels!" Deklan is now speaking to all of us who have gathered before him, before this sacrifice. "For eons, the perfect sacrifice has eluded your beings. Not through fault of trying, but fault of accomplishment."

If this is how he wants to start a peace treaty, I can assure you, it's not the way to do it.

"Today is a day for history among your kind. The included individuals participating in said sacrifice, will be returned their white wings, and be allowed to walk through the gates of heaven."

I hear whispers among the group of fallen. Some people I know, others I've never seen before. But every single one is gripping onto Deklan's words like they're written in stone.

Which, they may be.

"Now, don't be deceived. The situation in front of me may not be the perfect sacrifice. For the clouds only opened for our arrival because today was the day. These men in front of me," I don't miss the way he lingers on Mekaia's figure for longer than anything else in this world. "May die for no reason."

More murmurs and more whispers followed by some fallen leaving, giving up on the hope of ever getting back there. Well, they can have whatever was left of mine. I don't want to be some pompous prick who throws people from their home for love.

I have my love, and I'm not letting her go. For all of eternity, she will be mine. I will find a way.

This also brings up the question, how does Mekaia know Deklan? I know he's the only one who retained his memories, but why does Deklan seem so troubled by his appearance? Who are they to each other? Mekaia told me about his love and how he lost them, could that be Deklan? Were they close friends in Heaven?

So many questions run through my head and I'm scared I'll never be able to ask Mekaia. Usually, I can tell how battles are going to go. Technically, Mekaia is already captured, and against an army of heavenly, I'm not sure I will be able to do this on my own.

I scout the fallen and I can't see anyone who would risk their own life for Uriah, let alone Mekaia. Those who cannot remember do not feel the urge to fight against a system that prays on our downfall.

"Who is the soul who makes this offering to the Heavens?"

I look around slowly, eying everyone in the crowd. Show yourself. It doesn't take long until someone's wings spread and reveal the gray complexion Samara told me. Their feathers are falling out and they seem to barely be able to lift their owner. The person flies in front of the crowd and is just out of reach to see who they are.

"I am." Their voice is demonic, obviously hiding their true nature, but not their intention.

"I am the fallen, who wish to return to their rightful homeland that was taken from them." This person earns some feedback from the rest of the fallen, cheering them on, ready to go home. "I have brought before you two perfect sacrifices. Ready at your mercy to be brought to their end, so we, the fallen, may have a new beginning."

Cheers erupt from the crowd and I try to yell over them with no avail. "That's your leader!" They tune me out, drawn in by the power I feel off the culprit of these murders, over hurting Rose, over kidnapping and harming Uriah and Mekaia.

The person I'm going to kill.

I'm going to rip out their throat and let them watch as I tear open their insides, letting them leak out how their victims did. Until I rip their eyes out and let them feel the emptiness. Until I end their pathetic life. Rage builds up inside me as the culprit lowers their hood and stands tall in front of Mekaia and Uriah, facing Deklan and the Heavenly.

She takes off Mekaia's chains and he rises, the scars on him healing instantly. He laughs and I feel the bile in my throat rise, tears prick my eyes as he addresses us. "Fallen! Welcome, to our retribution!" Time stops around me almost like it did with those humans, I feel frozen in the middle of the square.

"If the heavenly do not accept our sacrifice, we will wage war! For our right to our true home, not here on Earth." Samara was right, it is Mekaia. He's fallen off the deep end, and he's taken Rose with him. They stand in front of me, staring in my eyes, practically beckoning me forward with them.

"Rowan," Rose is the first to speak, her normal green eyes are red with blood, just like Mekaia's.

"Rowan," He speaks over her, pulling out the tone that lets me know, this isn't a choice, "Those who support us in the perfect sacrifice, will receive reentry to Heaven, and will have their white wings returned to them." Mekaia reaches his hand out to me. "Rowan, you can go home. We can go home together."

Part of me wants to reach out and meet his hand. To go to our birthplace with him and forget about all the lonely years here.

No, not all were lonely.

I catch myself before our hands connect. "I will not leave Samara, and I will not allow you to kill my friend." Mekaia frowns, and Rose glances at him from the corner of her eyes, seemingly judging his reaction.

"Rowan please." He actually begs me, and pleads with his eyes. *No*, something's wrong. This isn't Mekaia. I take this time to slam my body into Rose and knock her over.

"Tell me what she's doing to you." I whisper to Mekaia quickly enough to get a response.

"She's threatened him." I glance back up to Deklan, watching the scene unfold and trying to hide his contradictions at our actions.

The person I trusted, for years. Someone I shared my body with, the body that belongs to Samara. This would be an honor for Samara, killing Rose. Killing the serial killer who has lost her mind and is threatening Mekaia to gather the support of the fallen. She wants to wage war, she wants destruction, she wants to go home.

What's most saddening of all, is that I'm going to take all of that from her.

THIRTY NINE

Samara

It's not long after Rowan left that I am pacing back and forth between the large windows in his apartment, carefully watching Central Park, waiting. I don't know what for. Rain pours down on the windows and yet my vision is clear, waiting for any movement, any sounds. "Sam?" Camille's voice makes me jump and I turn around to see her sitting criss-cross on the bed, staring up at me.

"Are you okay?" Her chocolate eyes gaze up at me, worry fills my chest. Everything since the day of the first murder, meeting Rowan, learning the truth, it all has led up to this very moment. The moment where I decide if I want him to take the risk of everything, or if I want to help him.

"Camille, I need you to stay here." I start grabbing a coat from his closet and making my way to the door while Camille gets up and stands in front of it, blocking my way.

"Absolutely not." Her tone is hard and demanding, she knows she won't let me out of this apartment, even if she has to fight me to do so. Camille and I have never been in a hands on fight before, but for Rowan I think maybe I would start one.

"Camille. Let me through."

She shakes her head, "No. It's dangerous enough for Rowan going into a fight he knows he has a disadvantage in. Imagine him being distracted by you." I shake my head and begin to pace again. I agree with her, but the emotions rolling through my body from Rowan tells me things look a lot worse than we think. The hair on the back of my neck stands up and I turn back to Camille. The door behind her opens slowly and silently, revealing a black hooded figure sliding through and grabbing Camille from behind, by the neck. I lunge forward, not sure what I would actually be able to do if I get a surprise attack on them.

Which I don't. They switch Camille over to the other side of their body and then throw their foot up to kick me. I fall to the ground, clutching my abdomen that is now throbbing in pain. They pull out something from under their jacket, the black dots that litter my vision make it hard for me to see what it is. Until they push it against Camille's neck, effectively making her go limp in their arms. They drop her to the ground, not gently, and stare at me for a moment before stalking over. Throwing the syringe down and grabbing a new one from under their jacket once more. I lift myself up onto my elbows and try my best to pull myself away from them, backing up all the way to the glass door, watching them stalk me slowly. They know they've won, that there's no where I can go. They're a predator and I am their prey, it's the last thought before they grab me and stick me with a different needle. The world around me fades to black and I feel Rowan slipping away from me.

My eyelids squeeze shut from the bright light that illuminates Central Park. Whoever grabbed us from Rowan's apartment put us on top of a building that overlooks the park. I can see hundreds of people, angels, down there. I try to find Rowan, but I should know better. I am simply human, maybe he could've used his supernatural abilities, but I can barely pass a vision test at the eye doctor.

I take some more time to focus on the heavenly angels that are standing front and center. They are truly beautiful, their wings are white as snow and I find myself blinking away the brightness as my eyes adjust. "Sam?" I hear Camille's voice and my head snaps away to see her parallel to me, laying on the ground.

"Camille!" I should get up, but I feel an aching in my neck, probably from where the needle was injected.

"Where are we?"

"Somewhere we aren't supposed to be." Answering Camille's question with unease in my voice, I glance over to where I can see the fallen and the heavenly. They look like they're about to face off. Which isn't too far off when I see someone get thrown to the ground. That red hair, Rose? I thought Rowan said she was hurt. I try to focus harder on what's going on below me. It doesn't take me long to hear shouting and then it's like all Hell breaks loose.

I actually mean it, the fighting that ensues makes the ground of the park crack open, revealing fiery lava. I can feel the heat radiating on top of the building we're on. I wonder what's going to happen when all of this is over? Will the Earth repair itself? Or will this be one of those stories that CNN can't solve? "Sam!" Camille's scream behind me snaps me out of my own thoughts and turns to see a dark hooded figure coming up the side of the building, right towards us.

I want it to be Rowan, coming to rescue us and get us out of here, but in my heart I know it's a much worse answer. "Camille, we have to go!" I haven't taken the time to actually look at Camille and see how she is. Her head is bleeding slightly but she doesn't seem disoriented, probably hit it when she fell or was laid down on this building. I grab her hand and help her stand up, running–more like jogging with the darkness dampening our vision–I hear a *swoosh* behind us and know that it might be all over.

We barely make it to the door on the roof that leads to the stairs before whoever is behind us grabs us, their arms wrapping around us with ease. Camille screams and I fight against them. "Sam stop!" I do as they say and my shoulders relax.

"Marcus?" The presence of the werewolf calms me down, but I have to relay that to Camille before she passes out.

"Camille!" I yell at her, drawing her attention to me, "He's a friend." She takes a couple deep breaths and I want to run and take her away from all this. Her life has been so scary for someone as young as her, and it feels like I'm only making it worse by getting involved in the supernatural.

"What are you doing here?" Marcus looks older for some reason, he's taller and he's even getting some scruff on his face. How could he change like that in such a short amount of time? There are so many questions from the supernatural that I have yet to begin to understand or even discover. "Rowan gave me a heads up when this started." Hearing his name makes my chest pang. Why can't I feel him? What's actually happening down there?

"He wanted me to take care of you and Camille." My heart pounds and I look at Camille who has the same look on her face. Except the main thing that concerns me is that her nose is bleeding. I cup her face and wipe her nose with my sleeve.

"Camille, are you alright?" Her eyes are wide and she reaches up to do the same to me. "Are you?"

Blood coats her sleeve and I realize that we may be in bigger trouble than we thought. "I'm sorry I couldn't protect you." I can't help but feel like I'm to blame for some of this. "Take me to Rowan." Marcus looks between me and Camille, reflecting on her by shaking his head. "Absolutely not." I scoff and turn back to Camille, who is clearly scared out of her mind, and while it might not make it any easier, we can try to get to Rowan and get the hell away from all of this.

"Marcus, take me to-"

"Samara, no!" His voice is deeper and there's a certain level of dominance displayed in it. If Rowan was here, he'd probably rip out his throat for talking to me that way. "You and Rowan are soulmates." I nod, following the conversation so far. "Do you remember the night we met, and I told you that I was looking for my mate?" I continue to nod. "I found her."

I smile softly and take in his appearance. I wonder if that's why he looks older and more mature? The supernatural part of him has found his other half, that has to have some kind of effect on him. For a split second, I don't worry about Marcus or Camille or Rowan, I become curious if any characteristics of mine have changed since meeting Rowan. Do I look more mature? Is my hair longer? Is my body language more elegant? The only thing I feel is complete with Rowan, whatever else happens must stem from that.

"If anything happened to her, I would die along with her." His words draw me back to him and also allows me to realize how dangerous this situation is. Rowan could die, Camille could die, I could die. "I am not letting you put yourself in danger for Rowan to risk losing you, losing it all." He's right but every particle of my being wants to cast all worries in the wind and run straight towards Rowan.

"What are we supposed to do?" I hear Camille's voice before my own, asking exactly what was going through my head. "We obviously aren't safe anywhere near here. You don't have wings to get us out of here and to run through, well that," She gestures towards the fighting as I try to take yet another glance to find Rowan. "Isn't the smartest idea."

Marcus nods to her and looks around. "You're right, I know. But we can't stay here, it's not safe."

"At least that's one thing you're right about." A new voice in the conversation, but not one in my head. She lands on top of the building, her red hair falls straight down, looking dead. Whatever she's been doing, it's been killing her.

Marcus takes a protective step in front of us, I try to hide the fear in my eyes but Camille's teeth are practically chittering out her mouth from how scared she is. Marcus in front of me, and me in front of Camille, each protecting the other with everything they have. Compared to Marcus, Camille and I have a lot less to offer in terms of protecting, but that doesn't mean we won't fight for each other.

"It's about time I got a hold of you."

"Leave her be, devil."

"Actually if we're getting technical, he's like my stepdad." She laughs and it sounds like nails on a chalkboard. I want to run. I want to grab Camille's hand and run. We can find Rowan and he can fly us out of here and away from everything.

"Move out of the way, wolf. This one and I have unfinished business."

"We never had any business to start with." I retort back to her when she points her finger at me.

"When Rowan decided to be with you, that's when our business started." Her eyes glow red and her wings look like they're disintegrating. She is literally falling apart as we speak.

"Just leave us alone." Camille says sternly, which surprises me, but I don't take my eyes off Rose, neither does Marcus. He knows if he does, it's a death sentence and that's when she will strike. Rose moves her head slightly to get a better look at Camille, and I instinctively try to block her vision. "You're the little squatter, I haven't had a chance to meet you yet. Why don't we all have a chat? Girl to girl."

Marcus pushes Camille and I back fast enough for us to get out of the way of her wings slicing through the air. Marcus is not as lucky. As Camille and I land on our backs, Marcus screams in agony. I look back up at him and suddenly the noise around us is too much to handle. I can smell the blood and feel the heat of the lava seeping through the earth. I can feel the footsteps pounding the ground and the wind has tousled my hair enough that I can feel debris in it. Marcus' whole chest is sliced open, it's a miracle he's still standing, but that's thanks to his supernatural abilities.

"Sam!" Camille grabs me by the shirt and starts pulling me. By the time I realize what is happening, Marcus has fallen to the ground and Rose is coming around him, straight for us. Running with Camille causes the adrenaline to rush my veins. I don't know if Marcus is alright but I do know that the edge of this building is coming soon. We slow slightly, not sure what to do when the edge of the building is in plain sight. I look over my shoulder and I don't see Rose anymore. She could be anywhere but she isn't behind us.

I grab Camille's hand and slow her down, to get a good look at our surroundings. "Where did she go?" I shake my head, she definitely did not give up, after all it seems like we are her true targets right now. By the time I turn and look back to the edge of the building, Rose is barreling towards. I hear Camille's scream before my own processes through the burning and stabbing I feel in my shoulder. Looking down I discover her claws have pierced the skin on my shoulder all the way through and are grabbing onto my back. The pain is enough to see black spots in my vision, and the only thing keeping me awake is Camille and her thrashing.

When that stops and Camille goes limp, my body slowly stops fighting and slips into limbo.

I wake up with a fright, thrashing and doing everything I can to find a corner and hide in it. The other part of my consciousness screams to find Camille. The last thing I remember is her lifeless body hanging down in Rose's arms, limp. I calm down when I realize where we are. We're on my apartment building roof, the fake grass and lawn furniture gives it away. Camille's on the opposite side of the roof from me, and her eyes are wide. There's no telling what thoughts are running through her head, but by the look in her eyes, they're probably on the same level with mine.

I don't see anyone on the roof with us, but I whisper to her, "Camille." She doesn't move or react, so I say it in a normal tone. "Camille." She shakes her head. She's scared to move. "Camille!" I yell, raising my voice at her is something I've never done more than a handful of times, but it does just the trick and snaps her out of her trance.

"Sam?"

I nod, "Everything's going to be okay."

She shakes her head and puts her hands over her eyes. "No, no, no, no!"

"Camille, calm down!"

She screams and thrashes, trying to break free of whatever they have us tied with. "They're going to kill us!"

She breaks down into tears and I do my best not to follow her. "I heard Rose and someone else talking, she's going to throw us off the building." Camille is terrified, and I feel sick to my stomach knowing there's not a damn thing I can do to protect her right now. Fallen angels begin to fill the roof, flying one at a time beside us. Many give me glares, but don't pay Camille any attention. I'm sure Rose has given them the soulmate run down.

Most are probably envious, and pissed. I feel him, Rowan, he's nearby. The realization that right now might be the last time I see Camille starts to dawn on me, and I take this moment to grab her attention once more. "Camille." She turns and looks at me, fear in her eyes still apparent by the tears threatening to spill. "Under the bed on my side is a box. It's got numbers, paperwork, letters."

"What?"

"I need you to read the letters and give them to everyone that has one."

Her confusion turns into fear as she realizes why I'm telling her this. "Sam, no!"

"Camille, the paperwork to adopt you is in there. It's done, I just haven't sent it out yet." The tears fall but they aren't from her, they're from me. My cheeks are damp and I begin to sniffle as I continue. "Rowan will take care of you. He's here, I can feel him."

"Sam, you can take care of me. He will get us out of here!"

I feel something connect with the back of my head and then I hear ringing. Camille screams in the background as I feel someone bring their leg up to my stomach, kicking. Pull back, kick. Pull back, hit. I don't know how long it lasts, because of the blood loss from Rose's assault and now this, everything is blurry and I'm surprised I'm still conscious. Whoever was delivering the blows lifts me up so I'm standing.

I vaguely see the outline of the side of the building and bad memories begin to infiltrate my mind. I hear Camille instead of seeing, she's on the opposite edge, clawing to get away from the two fallen holding her still. Rose laughs, shivers crawl up my spine and the hair on the back of my neck stands up.

Whatever is meant to happen, it stops here. I feel him, so close it's like he's touching my face.

"Rose!" I hear him, his sweet voice ringing through my ears. He's out for blood. I pray for anyone who has laid a hand on Camille and I. They'll pay the ultimate price.

"Whatever business you have with them is because of me. Let's finish this!" I hear someone approach, my vision is still blurry and I can't tell who it is until they speak.

"Don't you get it Rowan, she is why we're here." Rose places her hand on my shoulders and squeezes, causing me to yell out in pain. I feel the blood begin to run down my side from the injury.

"Rose!"

Rowan's voice fills the entire city, and I feel the angels around me stiffen, even going as far as to take a step back. "You will die, a slow, painful death because of what you've done to her, to them." I know he's talking about Camille, and probably Mekaia and Uriah, too. He's so close but so far away, my heart aches thinking he may not make it in time.

I feel my body being lifted and Camille begins to scream. The wind from the edge of the building blows my hair, which is slowly drying from the blood, and I know I'm being held over the edge. "Pick Rowan, who would you like to save?"

No. Please, no.

"You can save your soulmate, and live with the hatred she feels for not saving her child." Camille is my child and I would sacrifice my life for hers, but would Rowan? "Or you can save poor little Camille, and risk losing the other half of our soul, forever." If I die now, Rowan won't have another lifetime to look for me, this will be it. I'll die here and everything I've ever wanted and worked for will be gone.

No, Rowan's fast. He can save both of us, I know he can. What if he can't? What if Rose has another trick up her sleeve to prevent this from going our way?

She is a devious, conniving lunatic, and it won't surprise me if she gets her way, and one of us dies. "Rose, I swear to God!" The only gasp I hear is someone behind me, whatever it means, it's not good. "Swear to him all you like, he won't help you."

"Any last words?" Rose goes up to Camille first, and if I had any strength left, I would be fighting to get to her, to separate them and help Rowan kill Rose. The only thing that comes out of Camille's mouth is a sob before she chokes out a few works.

"Sam, I love you." My eyes release tears like a waterfall but I hold back my sniffle. I have to be strong for the both of us, and I won't allow Rose to prey on our weaknesses like she's already done. It stops now.

"Aw, the little baby is scared. What about you, Samara?" Her voice returns to the demonic nature of her state and her footsteps walk over towards me. She grabs my chin, lifting my face towards hers, a faint outline in my vision. "Any last words?" I glance towards Camille, and then towards the darkness, where I assume Rowan is. I can't see anything that's not right in front of me. I won't be able to see their faces before I die.

"Rowan, pick Camille. Save her." I hear him start to disagree but I interrupt him. "She's a child, she has so much to live for! Let her love, let her live." The sobs escape me and I hear Camille crying too. I'm not sure what Rowan looks like, or what his composure is, but I know in my heart, he's torn. "I'm so glad that you found me this time around, and were able to show me the love I was missing out on." Sniffle, cry, sob. Not in that exact order, but the only thing I feel now is broken, and defeated. "I love you, Rowan. Please, save Camille."

The silence afterwards is deafening, no one speaks, and it sounds like no one even breathes, until Rose laughs, and her people follow her. "You think he's going to save both of you deep down, don't you?" Another laugh, this time, she's in my face. Even though I can't see clearly, I can tell she's losing her grip on reality. Her face looks like it's decaying and it would shock me if her wings still held her off the ground.

"Even if he doesn't save me," The confidence in my words takes her back, and she listens intently. "He will still kill you." Back to silence as no one dares to interrupt us.

She moves quickly, pushing the angel holding me out of the way, and sinks her claws into my already mutilated shoulder. I cry out in pain and I hear both Camille and Rowan yell out towards me.

"Got you now." Rose whispers sinisterly to me before my body goes limp and before I hear Rowan scream.

FORTY

Rowan

The fighting started quickly and in the blink of an eye, I had lost Rose in the chaos. Coward. Leaving after starting a war? Real leader material. Fallen angels are the first to move and start charging. My mind races as I see Mekaia and Deklan fighting, or really just holding each others' arms as they speak.

I can't hear the words that are said, the sounds of Earth splitting into pieces is enough to snuff my hearing. I don't have time to analyze their interaction because someone slams me into the ground. The steam from the lava flowing beneath the cracked ground burns my face. A heavenly angel holds me down by the shoulders, her body pressed on top of me with fear in her eyes. She's as scared as I am.

"You don't have to do this!" She screams at me. She's doing what she's been taught, my guess is she doesn't even know what she's fighting for.

"I don't want this anymore than you!" I scream back at her. I know I can take her on, but she's younger, clueless, and afraid.

It hurts too much when they die afraid.

We sit in silence, struggling over who should make the next move. I finally decide that it's my turn whenever I see the dead, gray wings flying through the sky. Rose is trying to take away what I've worked for. Stability, friends, family, love, Samara. I cannot, and will not, let her take that from me.

I use my strength and flip us over so I am on top of her, my forearm by her throat. "Don't get up." The tone I use frightens her as her eyes grow wide and she gulps before nodding slightly. I get up swiftly and move away from the edge of the makeshift cliff. The angel listens, and she doesn't move. She's completely frozen with fear.

It's for the best, I think to myself.

Onto the main task at hand, I try to follow Rose through the warzone, but I get stopped every couple yards. Trying to dissolve violent situations is not in my resume, and it's hard to do it when they seem to be out for blood. They're the good guys, right? I think to myself but am simply reminded things aren't always what they seem. Heavenly angels gang up on the fallen and corral them to cliffs; forcing them to either jump into the lava or have their wings scorched trying to fly past.

The fallen play dirty and stalk the heavenly angels, ripping out feathers with their claws, making the heavenly panic and try to run. Predator and prey. That's all this battle is. Each side has their own fucked up feelings about our history, and this is how it always seemed to end.

A rush of panic washes over me and all I can think about is Samara. Where is she? Knowing her, there's absolutely no way she stayed in that apartment. However, to put Camille at risk? That's not something she would do. The panic leaves as quickly as it came, but it doesn't give me any relief of my own, as I wonder where her conscience is at.

I can usually sense her sitting in the back of my mind, sharing emotions with me, sending me pictures through her mind. When I try to focus on her, I can smell her vanilla scent and see the green of her eyes. Right now, I can only see darkness and smell the blood from the battlefield. I have to find her.

"Rowan!" I turn to see Uriah, beaten and bloody, stumbling towards me. His wings barely exist anymore.

"Uriah, what happened?" I lead him to the edge of a hill, hiding us from the battle as I check to see what I can help with.

"Those bitches jumped me." Looks like they were learning to not play fair either. "They took turns holding me down and pulling out my feathers." His voice cracks but he doesn't cry. Our wings are an extension of our souls, I know this hurts him more than I can imagine.

"Rose has the girls." I freeze and stop my checkup of him and lock eyes with him. "What did you just say?" He takes a deep breath, this conversation can go many ways, but they're all going to end with Rose dead. "I saw her grab them, I'm not sure if they're al-"

"Uriah, so help me God if you say dead, my face will be the last thing you see." I don't miss the way he glances at me as I pass over saying 'God', usually our throats burn, but mine doesn't. There are too many things rushing through my head at the moment.

The cries of battle begin to lessen and I peak over the hill we are hiding behind, the Fallen are moving further into the city and the Heavenly are chasing after them. "Where did she go?"

Uriah shakes his head, "Your guess is as good as mine." I look down at him, my friend who I have lived through many centuries with, he doesn't look like he's going to make it. "Don't get soft on me, go get your girl. I'm alright." The cuts and bruises that line his skin don't go unnoticed, and neither does the thick, red blood that is leaking from his shoulder blades. His body can't take much without his wings in great condition.

His body is trying to heal too many things at once, and it's not doing it appropriately. I take off my jacket and lay it over him. He's shivering, not a good sign. I don't want to leave him. I want to be here as he passes into whatever death holds for us. I don't want him to experience that alone. But, Samara could already be dead or fighting for her life with Rose. She won't last half a second compared to Uriah now.

"Don't you die on me. Last just a little longer for me okay?" He nods and holds his hand out, with whatever strength he has left. I accept it, knowing he is going to listen to what I'm asking. As soon as he drops his hand, I am following the rest of the battle further into the city. The destruction left behind, cracks in the earth, cars upside down, buildings destroyed, this is not what the fallen wanted. It's what Rose wanted.

She wanted this destruction, for what, I'm not sure. The sacrifice was not their original plan, so I'm guessing that a part of the story is missing. Why would the heavenly angels stay and fight if they knew this wasn't the right sacrifice? Why go through all of this trouble just to lose your people and cause destruction on Earth?

The panic rushes through me again and I take this time to propel forward with my wings. A new sense of urgency and realization surrounds me, and it's Samara's feelings that are clouding my thoughts. Wherever she has woken up, she's been there before and is comfortable. I look in the direction of where the battle is leading, and it stops in front of Samara's apartment building.

I go to my normal spot on the building in front and get a good look around the apartment. I see nothing out of the ordinary. Wine glasses in the sink, takeout on the counter, bed made, lamp on. It is just how she left it, how she always leaves it.

If they aren't in the apartment, then where exactly are they? I hear a high pitch scream and know it's Camille. The rooftop I am on is clear, but the building Samara lives in has multiple fallen, some holding Samara and Camille apart from one another on different ends of the building. They both look so tired. Camille is so frightened she can't move, and Samara is bleeding from her shoulder, her skin pale. God, what have they done to you?

I hear Rose laugh and the fallen on the roof make a path for her. She is sick. Her nose bleeds and her wings decay, whatever is happening to her is finally taking its toll. "Rowan!" Mekaia's voice triggers me to find him, always searching, always wondering where he is and what can I do to make his life easier. At least, that's how it's always been. Not anymore.

It doesn't take me long to find him being brought forward by Rose's lackeys, along with Deklan. Beaten and bloodied, no doubt from just being heavenly.

"Rose!" Addressing her must take her by surprise. She steps forward, waiting for whatever reason I have to say. "Whatever business you have with them is because of me. Let's finish this!" She walks closer to Samara and my stomach turns into a knot.

"Don't you get it Rowan, she is why we're here." She puts her hand on Samara's shoulder and squeezes. Hearing Samara scream seals her fate right then and there.

"Rose!" Drawing her attention back to me, I decide to remind everyone standing with her the reason I am second in command only to Mekaia. "You will die, a slow, painful death because of what you've done to her, to *them*." This is for myself, Mekaia, Uriah, Camille, and especially Samara. For her, I would do anything. I can save them, I might not be able to take on every fallen standing behind Rose, but taking her down and rescuing Samara and Camille won't be that much of a challenge. I just have to worry about their health status', they're human and it looks like both of them have already been injured. If I'm not careful, I could make it worse.

Rose motions with her hands and two of each of the Fallen come up and hold both Samara and Camille over the edge of the building, which just made this recuse mission twenty times more complicated.

"Pick Rowan, who would you like to save?"

What?

Rose motions to both of them as she stands between them. Camille is panicking and Samara just hangs there, almost lifeless. "You can save your soulmate, and live with the hatred she feels for not saving her child." The thought of Samara being here without Camille after how hard she's worked to make this adoption go through, how many hours she's spent with Camille, the girl who literally saved her life.

"Or you can save poor little Camille, and risk losing the other half of our soul, forever." Samara, I just found you. I will not lose you.

"Rose, I swear to God!" Deklan and Mekaia look up towards me quickly, whatever that was about, Deklan will not stop staring me down now.

"Swear to him all you like, he won't help you." I cannot wait to kill her.

"Any last words?" Rose asks Camille first, who is now a puddle of tears as she croaks out the only words she knows right now.

"Sam, I love you." Rose chuckles her reply and moves to Samara. The water prickles my eyes as tears threaten to spill and my throat feels like barbed wire is around it. I can't cry, if Camille and Samara see me cry they will think it's over. I will save them.

"Aw, the little baby is scared. What about you, Samara?"

Watching her, her Raven hair matted to her head from blood, her hazel eyes that look lifeless. She's tired. I'm going to save her, she will forgive me for not picking Camille, I cannot lose Samara again. If I lose her, this world will be subject to my damnation, and I pray for each and every soul that walks this Earth if she is taken from me.

"Rowan, pick Camille. Save her." Samara's voice is soft, I go to interrupt, knowing that it would hurt

Camille, but Samara stops me. "She's a child, she has so much to live for! Let her love, let her live." My guilt bares its ugly face, two seconds ago I was all for letting Camille die, the girl who protected Samara and threatened me with a butcher's knife just a couple weeks ago. What kind of person am I?

I know I'm not a good person, but I'm also not a monster, like Rose. "I'm so glad that you found me this time around, and were able to show me the love I was missing out on."

Samara, please.

"I love you, Rowan. Please, save Camille." Samara, my love, please don't make me choose. I have to save both of them, there's no other way for this to go.

I listen to Rose, she laughs and leans in close to Samara. "You think he's going to save both of you deep down, don't you?" I will. I'll save both of them, and take care of you.

"Even if he doesn't save me," Samara starts speaking, and I know I love her more and more each time she opens her mouth. "He will still kill you." *That's my girl.*

It brings me joy, but I know she is testing whatever patience Rose has left. By the looks of it, our time just ran out. Rose moves fast, switching spots with the angel holding onto Samara and sinks her claws through her shoulder. Samara screams out and I can tell life is slowly draining from her. "Got you now." Rose says in her demonic voice.

I watch in slow motion as Rose throws Samara over the edge of the building, the other Fallen throw Camille off right after. I scream and spring into action, flying as fast as I can towards them. They're on opposite sides of the building, and it's like they were thrown instead of just dropped. They're falling fast, Camille is screaming and Samara is silent, just falling. Everything moves so slowly I can see the droplets of the rain that are beginning to fall once more. I can hear the chambers of my heart fill with blood and pump, I can feel my pulse throughout my whole body.

What I can't feel is Samara's mind. I don't see, smell or hear anything from her consciousness, and I think the worst. My wings push forward through the air, cutting it in half to get to Camille first. She flails throughout the air as she falls, and eventually stops moving and goes limp. She's passed out and is headed towards the ground. I cut around the edge of the building and grab her lifeless body, half heartedly expecting her to wake up and cling to me.

Knowing everyone, especially Rose, up top is waiting to see if I can get both of them, I barrel through the glass wall in Samara's apartment and toss Camille on the bed, she will be fine. Using every ounce of my strength, I propel out of the bedroom and straight towards Samara. She falls with her back to the ground, and her hair swirling around her face. I can't see her eyes, I can't tell if she's alright.

Tucking my wings to go faster, the ground is right there, moments away. I can't miss, I have to grab her and fly up to prevent us from hitting the ground this fast. Even if I encased her inside my wings, she wouldn't survive it.

Lights pass by me and I do everything in my power to focus on nothing but her. Her raven hair, her red lips, her green eyes, her irresistible laugh, her warm body, the way her voice says "I love you." I can't be without her even for a moment. An eternity without her is my death sentence.

I feel the skin from her hand on mine, gripping it like my life depends on it. I pull her into my arms the same time I expand my wings, letting the wind carry me upwards, back towards the roof. The weight on my heart feels like a feather now that she is in my arms. "I knew I'd get you both." Finally reaching the top of the roof, I'm holding her bridal style, taking this time to observe her face. Her mouth hangs open and her eyes are closed. Blood lines the corners of her face and I know she has been through so much without me by her side. Never again will I be anywhere but by her side. I have waited an eternity for my forever, and I'm not letting it go anytime soon.

The roof is littered with remnants of the fallen angels who were here. Mekaia and Deklan are still here. Close enough to one another to find comfort, but far enough away to not be suspicious. I hear a sinister laugh coming from around the building, Rose.

Her body is weak, her attempt at reentering Heaven, unsuccessful.

"It's over Rose. You lost."

She throws her head back laughing, "Did I?"

The ground shakes, and the light from Heaven seeps down, lighting up the world.

Deklan is the next to speak, "But how?" I look towards him and Mekaia, who is looking at me with sad eyes. I don't understand until Rose speaks again. "Sacrificing one's true love might do it."

FORTY ONE

My heart begins to race as Rose continues to laugh in my face. Deklan finds enough strength to stand and face her, holding her into place for me. She's extremely weak, her eyes are bleeding now and her wings are slowly shrinking.

"You've been gone a long time, Rose." Deklan speaks, besides Mekaia, he is the one with the most knowledge about what this means. They begin to speak and I try to catch bits and pieces while listening to Samara's heart. I tune everything out and focus on it as hard as I can. It gets slower and slower, my breaths match it. I sink to my knees as I hold her close to my chest, watching her face.

Is she scared? Can she even feel me here anymore? What is she thinking? I put my forehead to hers, and breathe slowly, wanting to feel her breath fan my face to prove that she's still her.

When my skin touches hers, it's cold, with little to no fire left in it. "Please." I don't know who I whisper to, as far as I'm concerned, Samara and I are the only one's on this roof. As I'm about to pull back, something tells me to stay, just for a second longer, and I'm met with an image of her beautiful face, no blood or bruises and full of life in her eyes, smiling back at me.

"I love you, Rowan." The sun shines and the birds chirp, it's our perfect morning.

The image slowly turns dark and disappears, and so does her heartbeat, until it no longer beats. A strangled sob comes from my chest as I feel half of my heart stop beating. I can't breathe and my chest feels like it's closing in slowly, making me suffer the entire time.

She's gone, and she won't be coming back this time. I only had a glance at forever with her, and now I'll never get it again. My heart beats for her, my body moves for her, she is the sole purpose of my existence, and she's been ripped from me for the rest of my lonely eternity.

I try to memorize the beautiful dream she gave me and each second it slips further and further from my memory. I hold her close to my chest and turn her head into the crook of my neck, holding her close enough to never let go. I finally let go of the emotions I've been holding back, and I scream. So loud the building rumbles and the distant fighting comes to a halt. The light from Heaven dims only slightly before it opens more, and faster. The anger inside of me falters slightly into sadness, into a compromisable emotion.

No, I am not that person, I am a monster, I am a fallen angel and I will be the one who kills Rose. This pisses me off. Rose gets what she wants, and the only person I was ever meant to live for is gone. Ripped from this world like a toy from a child. Rose has taken my heart out of my chest, stomped on it, and tried to put it back into my body.

I hear heavy breathing, chuckling and sniffling. All three come from different people. The tears in my eyes vanish when I look at the situation in front of me. Mekaia is crying softly, his eyes never leaving mine, Deklan is trying his best to restrain Rose, who is laughing her head off.

She's proud of herself, for taking the other half of my soul, and she's about to regret every choice she's ever made since she landed on Earth. "Mekaia," I don't make eye contact with him, and my voice promotes authority like never before. "Hold Samara, do not put her down or I will rip your wings from your body."

"Yes sir." Mekaia says and I don't bat an eye. Things are changing around here, and this is the start.

"Deklan," Deklan looks over his shoulder and his eyes grow wide. I don't care what it's about. I have one mission on my mind right now. "Go check on Camille. Don't let her see Samara until I return." Neither of them look into my eyes, and I finish the sentence with, "Rose and I have business to take care of."

I leap towards her, my fist connecting with her stomach, allowing me to feel every rib I crack as we fly through the city. "You took *everything* from me!" A kick lands on her back where her wings meet her shoulder blades, and she screams as she flies further to the start of the battle. The wind stings my face from the tears that have been shed. Thinking about not having a home to go back to with Samara, sends me into a spiral.

I allow my wings to expand fully and let them cut through her skin, not deep enough to amputate her, but enough to cause discomfort and not allow her to escape. I grab her by her wings and throw her down to the ground. Her landing causes an eruption of dust as she lays there lifeless, barely breathing, and holding on for dear life.

"I'll do the same to you. Bit by bit. Allow you to watch as I dismember you and feed you to the dogs."

The fear in her eyes is present, but she can't move away from me as I stalk towards her. I'm the predator now. "I can't wait to rip the wings from your body and watch the life slowly fade from your eyes, just as Samara's did. You will wish you had killed me instead."

I don't expect her to say anything, or to plead, but she surprises me once again. "Rowan, we did it."

"Did what?" She motions behind me, specifically to my wings.

"Look." I don't trust her, I don't want to look away for one second. That might give her plenty of time to attack, but I let my curiosity get the better of me. Turning my head slightly, there's nothing going on behind me, but my wings are standing up and present, and they're different. Instead of the dark, deep black that surrounds my daily aurora, I'm now covered in a bright, holy light as my wings have changed to white.

"What did you do?"

I snap my eyes back to Rose, who is on her last leg of life, and she shakes her head, "You did it, for us." I shake my head, still confused about what's going on. Has she actually lost her mind this time? "The perfect sacrifice was losing Sam-"

"Don't you dare say her name!" I interrupt her. Samara's killer doesn't have a right to speak her name, her beautiful name.

"Picking someone, Camille, before her, and losing her. Protecting her until the very end. That was the perfect sacrifice. We can go home now." She laughs and begins to cry. "That's all I wanted, was to go home. I didn't want you or Mekaia or Uriah to hate me. I wanted it for us."

She is sobbing with what's left of her energy and reaches up an arm for me. This is still Rose. I hold her hand and lean down close to her, putting my hand on her head, comforting her. "I'm so sorry, Rowan." Her saying my name creates a knot in my stomach. The last person to say it was Samara, and I'd rather keep it that way.

I stand abruptly and expand my newly found white wings. I can't say I like them, but I don't hate them either.

"Fallen angel Rose, you are hereby charged with treason against your leader and council. How do you plead?"

My voice booms and the remainder of the battle ridden angels, heavenly and fallen, huddle around us, watching and waiting. I hear murmurs when people realize it's me, but with white wings. I pay them no attention, Samara is about to get her retribution. A life for a life.

"Rowan, please."

"You are also charged with corruption of a soulmate bond, one law I am hereby implementing in this day and age. No one is to tamper with, destroy, kill, or ruin any verified soulmate relationship with another angel. Heavenly or fallen." This earns gasps from the heavenly angels.

It means we accept their soulmate bonds as fallen, as their leader, which I am appointing myself, even with my white wings, it means we accept them, and they do not have to live in fear of exile. I hear Rose sniffling and begging, but the only thing I am hearing is Samara's voice. "I love you, Rowan."

Taking a deep breath, the tears threatening to break over, I continue speaking, "You are found guilty of all these charges, and I sentence you to death."

Before anyone can object, I grab her wings and rip them out. It doesn't take much, they've been weak for who knows how long, and now they're practically severed tree branches. I don't miss how she looks at me, silently pleading for her life as I stare down at her. The feelings we once shared were gone the moment I met Samara, but any respect I had for her ended when she killed her. Her scream cuts off as soon as they disconnect from her, and her body goes limp. Pale and lifeless. As it should be.

A life for a life.

FORTY TWO

The following week was the most trying week in my entire existence. The only person to really keep me going has been Camille. We haven't spoken much, but small gestures let me know we have each other's back. The last time we spoke was the morning after when she woke up in the hospital. She didn't remember much after being on the roof, and I broke down trying to tell her what happened. She figured the rest out on her own when Samara wasn't there when she woke up.

She's not like the other teenagers. She doesn't act out, sneak out, cause a ruckus, do drugs or whatever else they do now. She just sits and stares, draws a lot of the time, and occasionally asks to get food. I know this will improve, because frankly I haven't been the best person to be around.

Deklan, Mekaia and I constructed a pact. After I killed Rose, one of my wings turned back to black, but the other stayed white. Mekaia supported my claim as the leader of the fallen, and Deklan suggested we have a conversation since it's evident many were confused on my intentions with being halfway accepted into Heaven.

I made it extremely clear that I had no intentions of going back to Heaven as a heavenly angel, or whatever I was considered now. However, I did make it a point to reevaluate the standard conditions in terms of being cast down. The fallen and heavenly angels will live in harmony, and can travel between worlds if they want to, no punishment, no permission required.

This not only effectively ensures peace between our kinds as we learn to live together once more, but might even be able to eliminate the barriers completely. Also, it will keep an uprising, like with Rose, from happening again. As the fallen can visit Heaven anytime they wish, even if in small doses, the madness will stay away.

Instead of cleaning out Samara's apartment, I decided to give up mine and let Camille have the comfort of her normal space. She's given me enough respect to let me continue to stay in Samara's bed. The smell of her shampoo still makes me wake up thinking she's beside me. My heart has actually grown colder; the physician from Heaven that we procured, told me it's a side effect of losing a soulmate forever. Your body temperature runs slightly colder, and you'll notice it more than anyone. A part of you is missing, the other half of your soul is gone, *forever*.

The sun sets behind the buildings and I take a deep breath. Tonight won't just be me missing her, tonight will be different. I haven't had the courage to read the letter she wrote me, or open anything that was left untouched. Camille read her letter the second she got home, unable to be without Samara's presence for a second. I wonder if she thought this was some sick joke, just like I did.

The windows in the room have been repaired and all the glass has been cleaned up from that day. It's almost like she never left, except for the godforsaken memories that cloud my eyes everytime I walk in. The rough edges of the envelope dry out my hands, and the strain in my throat returns as tears threaten to spill over.

The words in this letter won't change the fact that she's gone from this plane, for the rest of my existence. I don't let the tears spill. For the past week, which has felt like years, it's been the same over and over again. Wake up, miss her, cry. Make myself busy, miss her, cry. Come home, see Camille, cry. I'm shocked I have any tears left in my body to get rid of. I have to take care of myself, but I also have to take care of Camille, for Samara.

Taking a deep breath, I open the envelope, and feel the warmth from the words she's written to me.

"Rowan, if you're reading this letter, it means somehow along the way I didn't make it. It means that you weren't able to save me like you did with NightHawk or Camille with her Dad. It means our short time together ran out." The sobs I've been trying to hold in escape, and the tears that fall begin to litter the paper below me. I prop my elbows on my knees and lean over, continuing to read the words that are going to rip out my heart.

"The idea of the supernatural world is still confusing to me. The anomalies I understood growing up to be fairytales, are actually living right beside me. Not to mention, I'm half of your soul, written in stone. I didn't think I would ever find someone for me, something was always missing. You filled the empty piece inside of me." I never knew if she understood the severity of our situation. The way our bodies were carved from the same Earth, molded into one being and then separated. We are half of one, and now it's just me.

"It may take me a bit to understand the level of everything, especially the danger watching us, watching me. No matter what happens, I don't need you to feel like this is your fault. It's not. I know you did your best." More tears, more sobs. If only she knew that I actually saved her. I saved both of them, and if Rose had stuck to her word and allowed me to try and save both of them, they would both be alive, not just Camille.

"You are my love, my body breathes for you, my heart aches for you and my soul is yours. Every part of my being, every part of my existence on this plane and the next, craves you. Sitting here, writing this letter and just missing you, I know what you're going through right now is the most difficult thing someone can bestow onto you." Samara, if only you knew. If only you knew the research I've put into learning if the soulmate bond truly goes away, or just goes dormant until I can find you again. If only everyone knew the research I've done to learn how to commit suicide as a fallen angel, it's nearly impossible. Our nature prevents us from completing even the smallest cut on ourselves.

"The one thing I will forever ask you, is to take care of Camille. She is my pride and joy, and I hope even though the adoption will not be finalized, she will still consider me a guardian. I love her like my own, I wish we could've had our own, but consider her yours. Protect her with your life." The irony in the letter is that I did, I protected Camille with my life, with Samara's life. I completed the perfect sacrifice and I did what my beloved told me to do, and that was to save her child. I picked her wishes over my own, and it caused me to lose her. But, I can abide by this one request. I can forever protect Camille as my own. If Samara and I were able to have children, they would be protected and they'd look like her. They'd be full of life like her, and they would be naive to the unknown dangers of this world.

"The different planes of this universe have no way of keeping my love from you. The highs and lows of our time together, the mischief and the experiences in the late hours of the night. The way I thought I would have all the time in the world with you. I'm sorry we didn't." We could've had all the time in the world, and there's nothing I can do to bring her back. My chest aches, and I have chills running up and down my arms. There's no warmth left, nothing left to smile about or someone to be mischievous with.

"From the bottom of my heart, my soul, my being—I love you Rowan. Forever." The note ends with her signature paired with a heart, and I clutch the paper like my life depends on it. Frankly, it feels like it does. It feels like if I let go of the letter for a second, that I'll crumble into a million tiny pieces and forget every trace of her. Like that's possible.

Like I could forget the sound of her voice in the wind, or her hair in the dark of night. Like tuning out the chirping birds could ever make me forget her laugh. Like the turning colors of the leaves in fall don't remind me of her eyes, they're beautiful. *Were*. Were beautiful.

Camille anonymously sent Samara's article to Shapiro Informatics, and when news spread of her disappearance, Francis somehow pulled her weight and got it published. Of course, Francis received a letter, and she met with Camille, so she wasn't in the dark about what happened. For the most part. Francis had to finish the article and I haven't read it, but from what Camille tells me, it kept Samara her job. It also put the public at ease, knowing the killer at large was not a problem anymore, and that the police are there to keep them safe. At least, I guess that's what they believe.

Camille and I have decided to take a trip to Samara's small town in Kentucky. She wrote a letter for her Mom, and I'm sad to say I'm not sure when the last time they talked was. Camille says it wasn't too long ago, and that makes me feel better that she at least spoke to her before *it* happened.

The drive is quiet, like our life feels now. I know Samara wouldn't want it this way. She would want us to keep living, and the world that I'm creating between the supernatural and the mortal realm is going to help that. The sun is setting, and the sky turns to a beautiful orange color, highlighting the Angels that fly through the clouds. One looks familiar, raven hair blowing in the wind, with white wings that follow behind her. My heart grows warm, and feels like it beats faster. With this, I know: I'll find her in every lifetime. No matter how long it takes.

ACKNOWLEDGEMENTS

My first ever book being completed means so much to me. Never in my twenty-three years did I think I would be capable of something as amazing as this.

A special thanks to my parents, who listened to all the crazy ideas after dinner every night of what I envisioned for this book. Thank you to my Mom, for taking a leap of faith and going outside her normal genres to give my book a chance. Thank you to my Dad, who has probably never read a book since he graduated high school (more of a working man), it means so much that you can support me on this. I love you guys.

Though they may never read them, my dogs, Disco and Sugar, for being my companions in the late night ideas. Unfortunately, my chickens were a lot less involved in this than I wish. Although, the idea of the wings came from them, so they did enough.

My close friends and family, who had to suffer through my endless rambling when it came time to publish.

Sam at Fictional Fabrication, your kindness and experience when it came to editing my book made the process less daunting than what I was looking at back in 2020 when I started writing this. You were a joy to work with, and I hope more people will be able to see your amazing qualities. Thank you.

Everyone at Palmetto Publishing, thank you for being so patient with me. Living and working full time as a young adult living on her own is a most daunting task, and your understanding of my schedule to publish helped me realize putting myself first should be my number one concern.

Thank you all who had faith and supported me. This was a long time coming, and I am glad we are all here to see it.

ABOUT THE AUTHOR

Abbi Gore Spivey is a professional daydreamer, full time dog mom, and part-time writer who crafts stories about love, heartbreak, and the journeys that define us all.

She lives in Conway, South Carolina and has graduated from HGTC. When she's not writing, Abbi can be found lost in a good book, enjoying time with the people who matter the most, and sipping on a Dr. Pepper.

Her writing reflects the depth of her experiences in life–the joy of connection and the bittersweet nature of life and love.

Abbi believes that everyday is an opportunity to dream, and she's thrilled to see her book come to fruition.

www.ingramcontent.com/pod-product-compliance
Ingram Content Group UK Ltd.
Pitfield, Milton Keynes, MK11 3LW, UK
UKHW020700200225
455358UK00010B/518